I0784198

Disciple, Interrupted

Stories From Between the Lines

Sara Heacox Sosa

Copyright © 2023 Sara Heacox Sosa.

All rights reserved. No part of this publication may be reproduced, distributed, or transmitted in any form or by any means, including photocopying, recording, or other electronic or mechanical methods, without the prior written permission of the publisher, except in the case of brief quotations embodied in critical reviews and certain other noncommercial uses permitted by copyright law. For permission requests, email the publisher at the email address below.

ISBN: 979-8-9887232-1-9

Unless otherwise indicated, all Scripture quotations are taken from the *Holy Bible*, New Living Translation, copyright © 1996, 2004, 2015 by Tyndale House Foundation. Used by permission of Tyndale House Publishers, Carol Stream, Illinois 60188. All rights reserved.

Editing by Ink Drinker Editing and Literary Services | inkdrinkerliterary.com
Cover layout by Heather Paul | artofheatherpaul.com
Interior layout by Ink Drinker Editing and Literary Services | inkdrinkerliterary.com
Cover art: "sola ossa," oil on canvas, by EK Sosa | @ramblebramble.ink
Author photo by Peter Heacox | heacoxphotography.wordpress.com

First printing edition 2023.

Sara Heacox Sosa

Advance Praise for Disciple, Interrupted

They say a friend is someone who learns the song you sing, then sings it to you when you have forgotten. Sara has learned deeply the song of the Gospel, told through so many characters she has intimately befriended. And now she shares that song in this beautiful retelling of the Gospel story. You shall be enriched and reminded.

Wayne Park, Chancellor, Fuller Theological Seminary Texas, and Assistant Professor of Congregational and Marketplace Leadership

Life is a struggle and sometimes it becomes difficult to overcome our struggles by ourselves. We need someone who can understand our situation and help us with our struggles. Dr. Sara Heacox Sosa in *Disciple, Interrupted* narrates from the Gospels the stories of those people who had different kinds of struggles but whose lives were transformed for the best after their encounter with Jesus. These Gospel stories are narrated in a very captivating and dramatized way that it will be difficult to put it down once you start reading. They are so down to earth and you will start to say, "that is me." You will feel the love, compassion, understanding, and kindness of Jesus to those who are in some kind of life's struggle. You will never regret reading this book.

Frew Tamrat, PhD
Principal, Evangelical Theological College, Addis Ababa, Ethiopia

In this work, Sara Heacox Sosa has brought to life the stories of ordinary people in Scripture who encountered Jesus. It is beautifully written and will transport you into the heart and mind of the people Jesus touched, healed, served, taught, and at every turn, discipled. This book will invite you to a richer, fuller, deeper experience with Jesus, the Great Interrupter, and maybe...just maybe...your life will be interrupted too!

Denise Muir Kjesbo, Ph.D.
Professor and Program Director
Master of Arts in Children's, Youth and Family Ministry
Bethel Seminary, St. Paul, MN

I loved this book!! In these pages, Sara brings life to the Biblical stories many of us have read for years. Through her insightful, personal approach to the "back story", she adds richness and depth to the power of people encountering Jesus and being changed by his love. If you want some fresh eyes on these stories, then *Disciple, Interrupted* is the book you should be reading.

Tiger McLuen, Executive Director--Youth Ministry Consultants. www.youthm inistryconsultants.org

Contents

For Emma & Matteo...

My life's undeniable truth
is Jesus;
My life's biggest honor
is being your mom;

Both have inspired these stories.

Jesus predicted it himself: "The children of this world are often more clever than the children of the light" (Luke 16:8) which is probably why he made the sinner, the outsider, the Gentile, the Samaritan, the woman, the Roman centurion, the poor person, and the leper heroes and heroines of his stories.

Richard Rohr
Falling Upward: A Spirituality for the Two Halves of Life

Introduction

I often wonder what it would have been like to have Peter as a brother.

There are many stories in the Bible that include Peter, showcasing his bravado and zest for living. There was the time he insisted on walking on water (because Jesus was) and ended up sinking because, well, he's not Jesus. Or the time he tried to stand up for Jesus in the garden by drawing his sword and cutting someone's ear off! Both times, Peter needed Jesus to pull him back from his impetuous actions. That was simply Peter. But Andrew? All he gets is a few small mentions in Scripture, but those mentions give important insight into one person around Jesus who intrigues me the most.

In John's Gospel, we learn Andrew is the one who met Jesus first. As a result, you would expect him to shine a little more, and share the stage with Peter more often. On the contrary, Andrew stays on the sidelines, a quiet presence in the stories where he appears. It will be Peter who forms the more visible friendship with Jesus. In fact, Jesus vows to build his church on Peter. I can imagine Andrew quietly saying to himself, "But I found him first."

And that's just it. I imagine Andrew is the classic introvert, and his brother is the quintessential extrovert. As an introvert myself, I empathize with Andrew. Where Andrew fades into the background of the story, Peter is the very fabric from which the story is made. It's easy to picture Andrew's life as lived mainly in the shadow of his gregarious brother. That must have been a bittersweet place to grow up. Even so, it seems that Andrew admires his brother, and their relationship is close. After all, it's these two brothers often listed with two other brothers (James and John) as the top foursome of Jesus' inner circle. All fishermen, all friends, deeply connected to one another and, eventually, to Jesus.

My empathy and exploration of Andrew led me to many others like him in scripture. Over thirty-six others who felt overlooked, misunderstood, and unappreciated until they met the Living God. Thirty-six others whose lives were interrupted by a man who could see them and their needs in ways no one else could...or would. I found I longed to hear more from them. What were their fears, hopes, and gifts? If their stories were more fully revealed in scripture, would they have offered us a new and different perspective on faith?

With curiosity, imagination, and prayer, this book holds my humble attempts to hear from them. I encourage you to read these stories slowly, intentionally, the way you might read a poem. Let yourself feel the emotions of these people who encountered Jesus in life-giving ways.

May their confessions, disclosures, and testimonies remind you Jesus was ushering in an all-encompassing, radical love. A love that transformed culture, to transform people. With just one look, one word, or one touch, a deep love flowed through Jesus to others, even those who seemingly had little to no value.

Perhaps you have read this far and are still wondering if this book is for you? I hear you. I build my personal library very carefully too. So let's see...

Is this book for you?

What if I have given up on Jesus because the church, as presented in the media, isn't inviting?

If you truly want to be introduced to a Jesus whose heart yearns for all people to be seen and heard, you don't have to look further than the Gospels in the Bible. They clearly present the real and radical way of Jesus without apology. What we get through the media is a warped image of Jesus and a disappointing view of those who claim to follow him. Any expression of a church that excludes people from its fellowship in any way is simply not built from the truth of who Jesus was and still is.

What if I want to feel like I am part of a community, but don't like the label of 'Christian'?

You're not alone! Start by simply choosing to align yourself with Jesus. Study how he spent his time with people and endeavor to do the same. You don't need a label to advocate for people, to invest in people, or to love them well.

What if in the past, others have not understood my hurt?

Human beings are limited creations. But God, as the Creator, doesn't have those limits. By extension, neither does Jesus. What does that mean? It means that where others fall short in hearing, seeing, and understanding you, Jesus won't. He lived 33 years as a human being, feeling and experiencing each stage of life from birth into adulthood. Not only does he know about your hurts, he can feel them, too, and you'll experience this side of Jesus as you read this book.

What if my past traumas feel too big to move through and forgive?

There are several stories of people in this book who likely asked the same question. I think of the woman at the well, the woman caught in adultery, and the woman who spent her life savings to find a cure for a bleeding disorder.

You will likely see pieces of your story in theirs and perhaps feel comforted and hopeful. See how Jesus responded to each of them, meeting their physical needs and, more importantly, their emotional and spiritual ones as well.

What if my experience in a small group turned me off from reading the Bible?

Perhaps you would give these stories a chance? They help us imagine the backstory, the one that isn't described for us in Scripture. They are all based on real people and real stories from Scripture. Each demonstrates how Jesus, time and again, showed what it looked like to truly be present with others. I pray that as you give Jesus a second (or third, or fourth) chance that the pain from your past will be met with the redeeming love of Jesus.

Don't Forget Your Bonuses!

Before you read any further, I want to share two bonuses to enhance your experience in this book.

These bonuses will:

- Increase your confidence as they remind you of how Jesus sees you

- Add a splash of encouragement to your day through the beauty of art

- Captivate your imagination in sacred ways and

- Catalyze you to embody Jesus' love for others throughout your day

These bonuses are:

1. One-of-a-kind phone wallpaper based on the stories explored in this book by author Sara Heacox Sosa. With these, you can take encouragements from God with you wherever you go. Choose from seven different designs.

2. Printable art from stories in the book. Choose from six stories and receive a digital 8x10 art file that illustrates that story.

Both of these bonuses await you with the following link. Please know that your email is safe with me. :) I will never spam you nor sell your contact info. Sharing your email with me not only gets you these bonuses, but it also keeps you in the know of other ways that I can serve you in the future.

SECTION 1: HEAVEN CAME DOWN

More than a prophet and more than a king,
Jesus was with God in the beginning,
created all that is, and was now on earth
to offer his sinless life as a sacrifice for our sins.
Were it not true, such a belief
would be the height of delusion.
But the deluded do not act as Jesus acted.

Alicia Britt Chole
Anonymous: Jesus' Hidden Years...and Yours

1

CHOSEN TO SPEAK

- ISAIAH -

Isaiah 9:1-7

I believe in the coming of the Messiah. I struggle with the possibility that I may not see him in my lifetime. But I'm sure he is coming; God told me so.

I can't say I have always enjoyed my role as God's prophet. Sometimes, what God shares with me causes me to hold my breath. And in that moment, I am reminded that He is God, and I am so much less. It's a beautiful arrangement...this relationship...this dance. He could speak in his own right, yet he speaks through me. Sometimes, in the quiet of my prayers I ask, "Why? Why, God, did you choose me?" He hasn't answered that question.

I have other questions like, "Why should the God of all that I know care so much about us?" When I look at the nation of God, as I have seen it, I shake my head in frustration and sometimes disgust. They don't honor him. They don't revere him nor do they serve him. Why does God still pursue them?

But I know the answer—love. In my old age, there are some things that I have come to understand about love. Let me tell you about them.

Love is untamable. You may think you can control it, but in the end, love will rest where it wants. It doesn't wait for an invitation to come around.

Love is tenacious. You can turn your back and walk away, but love will pursue. When you tire of walking, you'll bump into it. Love will fight for your attention. It will do extravagant things to get you to notice. Love never gives up.

Love is restless. It's always on the move, always searching for a way in. Love won't force itself in, but when it's invited, it will stay—forever. Be prepared for it to make a home with you and change your life.

Here's the most essential truth...God is love. He is all the things I have just said: untamable, tenacious, restless, as he waits for his creation to turn in his direction. He waits for us. That's love. I know about God's love because he has shown it to me firsthand. He has told me about it through dreams. I have experienced it in real life. God has told me he is sending his love to the world in a new way. I dream of God with us.

I have a lot of words I could share with you about the coming savior—God's gift of love for all of creation. I know what we are told to call him as God has given him these names: Wonderful Counselor. Mighty God. Everlasting Father. Prince of Peace.

I'm unsure why God chose me to speak to his people, but he has. Of all the messages he has given me to share, this is perhaps the most important. I don't know the time or the exact place when God will choose to enter our lives, but I know he will.

He has told me that a time is coming when heaven will reach down and touch earth. God will appear in our world in a way he never has. There is mystery in the how and why. But I can say, with conviction, it will happen. I believe in God's love coming near. I believe in God coming to be with us. I believe in the coming of Immanuel.

2

Message Sent

- GABRIEL -

Luke 1:26-38

THE HOPE OF THE world is what Jesus will become. He was present with the Father and the Spirit at the time of creation. Now, he is moments away from becoming a part of that creation. I am astounded. There are innumerable ways that God could accomplish his will, but this is his choice. We serve a God who allows choice in his creation.

God will not force his way into their lives. He will not decide for them. From the very beginning, it has been so. And because it has been so, creation is a mess. Mercifully, God won't let it stay that way forever. But he won't make it easy, either. We have watched his creation for thousands of years. We have witnessed their tepid response to God's work among them. Based on that alone, I know this will not be easy.

It could have been.

We watched in silence as that crafty serpent tempted the woman and her husband. We longed to be the voice in their ears telling them not to listen to his lies, pleading with them to obey the only command they had been given. But God did not give us permission to intervene. God wanted them to choose.

They chose badly. In their sin, they had to be sent away from the Garden for their own protection. There was heartbreak throughout heaven as God banished the man and woman and placed one of our own to guard the entrance with a flaming sword. The separation began.

It would take hours to recount for you all the times since then that God has called to his creation to give guidance, reassurance, and an opportunity to return to his embrace. But their sin and unwillingness to trust in God kept them far from us. I do not know the future as God does. As close as I am to him, he does not tell me what is coming. We simply watch him devise ways to call to them, to chase them, to protect them. We have often been a part of that protection, though most people cannot see us, are not aware of us in their midst. Their hearts are hard and their eyes are blind. It is so frustrating because it does not have to be that way.

Yet, every so often, there are people who see us at work. Often, they are children...young ones with pure hearts. They can see us. They are not afraid of us. Some even talk to us. In my non-human form, I am enormous. Angels are bright and blinding and so much taller than humans. We terrify those who can see us, but not the little ones. They seem to know, to understand, that we are there on their behalf and that we represent the One in heaven who knit them together. Adults often cower in our presence, but children smile.

I am pulled from my wonderings about this quirky creation by the voice of God. He has called me to his side and so I go, eager to be of service to him if I can. His face is somber. His Son stands next to him. I hold my breath but then relax when I see the light that shines in their eyes. Hope.

There is nothing that extinguishes hope when you are in the presence of God.

I wait for him to reveal to me what he needs, and he does so without a change in expression. When I hear what he wants from me, I am excited, proud, and more than willing. I am also perplexed, in awe, and left wondering at the ideas that he puts into play. This one is particularly breathtaking. I gladly accept my role and his blessing as I turn to leave his presence. I am just steps away from him and I feel the distance already.

In no time at all, I am standing on earth...from the realm of the Creator to the world of the created in a breath. I am outside a small home in Nazareth...a little town of no consequence in the world of its day. But those who know the prophecies of God have been waiting for God to move. He is moving now, and I have the privilege of announcing his plan. I have been to a similar place recently. Only a few months back, I stood outside of a temple in the hill town of Hebron. As God's messenger, I brought news to Zechariah about the coming birth of a long-awaited child. To the barren couple, it was too much to believe. But it was the way God restored their hope.

The girl I will visit now is young. I know she will not be afraid of me. Even in my human form, she will know me to be a messenger from God. She will know that God is in the room. She will understand that something much bigger than anything that she could imagine is about to happen. And, just like me, she will count it a privilege to have a role in this new plan from God. I have come during her prayers and I listen as she pours out her heart to the God she loves. Words of compassion, of love, of obedience mingle with trust, with devotion, with hope. He has chosen well. I have come to expect no less.

The message I have been chosen to deliver is about to change her life, drastically. It will impact those she loves and change this town. It will change the entire world forever. God will call out to his creation in a way he never has before. I pray this time they will listen. I pray this time they will allow themselves to be reconciled to their Creator; the one who loves them so fiercely that heaven trembles. The Hope of the world is coming soon.

I walk into Mary's prayers to reveal to her that she will be the one to conceive, carry, birth, nurture, raise and release this hope for all of creation. I am ready, and so is she. I am Gabriel, God's messenger, sent to tell Mary she will bring this hope and Messiah into the world. It will not be easy. But she will not do it alone. God will be with her. The Messiah is coming...this is hope.

3

SILENT STRUGGLE

- JOSEPH -

Matthew 1:18-25

I LOVE HER. IT is the truth that keeps me tethered to this town. I could walk away if I were not so consumed and tangled in that love. But my love for her anchors me here as I wrestle through my pain and wonder when I will ever stop hurting. Tears spring to my eyes, and I blink them away as memories walk me through the past years of my life growing up in Nazareth with Mary. I pause at each one, reminded that I do not want to live my life without her in it.

Why do I care so much? Many young women in this town would be excellent wives. Perhaps I could choose one of them instead. But Mary is the one I want for my wife...the one I have chosen...the one to whom I am promised. There is a quality about her that differs from her friends. She is beautiful, yes. But more than that, she is a woman of complete integrity with wisdom, grace, and confidence. She is determined and sure, and filled with faith.

At least, she used to be. Until yesterday afternoon, I knew her to be all those things. Today, I am filled with doubts and questions and pain. We are to be married. It is all I have wanted for years. Growing up in the same village together, I knew God had put her in my life for a reason. Our friendship is strong. We have shared much of life together...laughter, tears, prayers, concerns, and a confident faith in our God who provides.

Faithful is not a word I would use to describe her now. After what she shared with me yesterday, I know she has not been faithful. She told me she was going to have a baby. I know it is not mine. We have shared many things over the years, but not the intimacy between a husband and his wife. That is a boundary I would never have crossed. I am shattered to find that she has.

Oh God in heaven! What am I to do? We have told no one else yet, but we must share it. And as soon as the town knows, they will punish her. They will cut her off from the temple, her friends, and her family...from me. She will be alone. The thought is crushing.

How can I watch that happen to her? Yet is it not the result of her actions? They will expect me to set her aside, to break off our engagement. The elders will call for her to be disciplined, and how that is done will be my choice. My choice. I don't want to make that choice.

Where are you, Lord? I have been crying to hear your voice in this, yet you are silent. I have heard nothing. Have I done something wrong that you will not whisper to my heart when I need your direction the most? Mary is a gift you gave me...now you would take her away? Have I not walked in your ways since I was a small boy? Have I not studied your word and committed it to memory? Have I not been dedicated to you? Still, I hear nothing. Your silence is a heavy weight that presses into me.

I could stand with her. I could allow people to believe an untruth—that the child she carries is mine. But it would be a lie. Others might not know, but I would. And God would. I wonder if I could do it. I allow myself to consider what life would be like between now and the birth of that child. And when the child comes, could I care for it as a father? Knowing every single time I looked at it would remind me the child is not mine even though the world would think it is? What would that take from me?

The energy building inside me is strong. I am trying my best to stay calm, but I find I want to run. I want to yell. I want to break something. This is too much. I am raw from the emotion that is consuming me. Tears are demanding release from my eyes and I struggle to hold out against what builds from within. It takes all my strength, but I cannot crumble now. Without the voice of God in my ear, I must be strong and make the best decision possible. I fight to push back the pain and I can feel myself gaining control. I am exhausted, so I lay down to sleep. Perhaps in the morning, I will better know what to do.

As I close my eyes, my conversation with Mary returns to me. I can see her face as she spoke to me. Strong. Steady. Her eyes pleaded with me to understand and believe the words that came from her mouth. But she told me something I know is impossible. She told me about the baby, but she shared so much more. She talked of a visit from God's messenger, an angel, come to her. I looked at the sincerity in her eyes and knew she was telling the truth. She would not lie to me.

Then she shared the angel's message—that she would find herself with child by the power of the Holy Spirit and God himself, and the result would be that she would bear the Messiah, the hope of the world, the proof of God's love. I couldn't process that. I could not get my head around it. I have grown up looking for signs of the coming Messiah. I have watched hope play across the faces of the men in the synagogue as they wait for God to send the Messiah to rescue us. It is a familiar theme, but I have always held it for the future. Never had the idea come so close.

It didn't make sense then, and it does not make sense now. A baby? How can a baby help us? This cannot possibly be God's best plan? Is it God? Is it your best plan? I think again about the woman I love. I cannot let her go, but I know I should. I want to believe what she shared, but I cannot. Tears finally spill onto my pillow as I realize that tomorrow I will say goodbye to the woman I love, the life I have built, and the God who will not speak, though I need him desperately.

As the world fades to black and heavy eyelids close, I suddenly hear a voice cut through the silence. "Joseph, son of David, do not be afraid to take Mary as your wife. For the child within her was conceived by the Holy Spirit. And she will have a son, and you are to name him Jesus, for he will save his people from their sins."

Reassurance and peace wash over me. God has finally spoken. I have one last thought as I give in to sleep...this is love.

4

Heart of a Mother

- ANNE -

Luke 2:1-5

I'm finally at peace. These have been long months full of tension. You see, I've watched my daughter Mary bear accusations that she is a liar. I have seen her almost lose her marriage to a man she loves deeply. I have stood by in silence as she endured anger from synagogue leaders, distance from childhood friends, and disappointment from her father. She has been unwavering through all of it, but I know that her father's disappointment is the one that has hurt her the most.

I love this girl God gave us years ago as a tiny, beautiful baby. I know her father deeply loves her as well. But the revelation of her pregnancy before her marriage to Joseph was more than he could handle. And I stood in the middle. Silently. I wanted to wrap both of them in my arms and bring them back together. I wanted to be the one to say everything would be okay. Instead, I said nothing.

How could I? I was not invited to speak into my husband's misery. He had the luxury of suffering publicly. I have been suffering privately. For nine months, I have stood at his side, genuinely offering my support to him while crying out on the inside for what has torn our family apart. No one would know...no one will know...what I have endured because I have said nothing.

I couldn't even speak to Mary. I wanted to tell her I believed her story and that the baby was of God. But until recently, I did not believe that. It was too outrageous to believe. We all know how babies are born. I was angry with Mary and Joseph for a long time. Angry that Mary had not waited until her marriage. And even more furious with Joseph for abusing the promises our family made to him.

I am not angry anymore. I realize that from the very first telling, their story hasn't changed. Mary's convictions of what happened and is happening in her life are as sure as the sun's rising and setting. Her devotion to God is undiminished—if anything, it has become more profound. Joseph was not so sure at first. But then, one night, he went from being on the verge of dissolving his agreement with Mary to standing unwaveringly by her side.

Through all of this, Joseph has been the gift that has taught me to believe. In addition to Mary's story of the visit of an angel was Joseph's story of God's messenger coming to him. The following day, Joseph found Mary and told her he believed her and, together, they would walk the difficult road ahead.

He has done just that. He has loved her in practical and extravagant ways. Together, they have experienced the awe and fear of a coming child. His voice has been soothing, encouraging, and loving. I have watched him love my daughter in a way I could not. It has been water to my thirsty soul.

Now they are gone. Just yesterday, they took our donkey for a long journey to Bethlehem. Because of the Roman census, he must go there to register for taxes. Although she is nine months pregnant, Mary has gone with him. I thought I would be terrified for her. In truth, she could have her baby along the road with only a young Jewish man to help her. No female relatives or a midwife. So many things could go wrong. I ought to be uncontrollably anxious.

But as I watched them move slowly down the road that led out of Nazareth, I found I was not afraid. I was hopeful. You see, I now believe—through Mary's conviction, Joseph's dedication, and God's grace—that my daughter carries the Messiah within her. It is that knowledge that assures me that all will be well.

God has chosen her. God has chosen Joseph. I have told God many times in the past months that he has chosen well. The Messiah is coming soon. I am at peace.

5

First to Hear

- SHEPHERD BOY -

Luke 2:8-20

I LOVE BEING OUTSIDE and being with these sheep. Sometimes it's hard work, like when they wander off, get stuck somewhere, or attract wild animals. And the days can be really hot as we walk long distances to get to water and fresh grass. At night, after we have gathered the sheep together for safety, I wander the hillside watching for danger and looking at the stars. And sometimes I watch the angels. I have seen them on the hillside with us many times. I'm not afraid of them, even though they are so big. Once, I told my dad about seeing the angels. He just looked at me like I was crazy. I guess his reaction didn't surprise me, but part of me was hoping he would say he had seen them, too.

The sun is setting, and I am getting the sheep settled for the night. I can see small lights from lanterns that have been lit in the city below. The city has been really busy this past week. People are coming to be counted by the government. I'm not sure why the Romans care how many people are in my village. Bethlehem is just a sleepy little town. I sit down, grab a piece of bread out of my bag, and take a bite.

As I chew, the hair on the back of my neck stands up, and the air feels electric. I know what this means because it has happened before. Suddenly, before me is a man dressed in white. He looks like a man, but

25

he shimmers and shines. I know he is an angel. No one else sees him but me.

I look at the angel and realize that I have never seen one this size. Usually, they are enormous and fill the sky, but this one is not much taller than me and he is watching me. So, I watch him. He moves to the side and my eyes follow him. He smiles, "You can see me." I jump as he speaks to me! Amazing.

"I have come to deliver incredible news," he says. I nod yes, but say nothing. He smiles at me, "Get ready."

He turns away from me and is suddenly the size of the other angels I have seen. This time—this time the other shepherds notice. They stop mid-sentence and stare with growing fear at this spectacle before them. They scramble closer together, eyes wide with fear. In a rolling thunder voice, the angel says, "Don't be afraid! I bring you good news that will bring great joy to all people." They crowd together, trying to back away from the angel. But I step closer...I want to hear this news.

"The Savior—yes, the Messiah, the Lord—has been born today in Bethlehem, the city of David! And you will recognize him by this sign: You will find a baby wrapped snugly in strips of cloth, lying in a manger."

My feet are already moving toward town. The Messiah? In Bethlehem? I run, not waiting for the others, barely hearing what sounds like a choir singing in the background. I am going to find this baby. I want to see him with my own eyes! Surely, he matters greatly if God sent angels to announce his birth.

6

CAPTIVATED BY A STAR

- GASPAR -

Matthew 2:1-12

THE NIGHT SKY. NOTHING in all my life has captivated me more. The stars are part of my family. Growing up an only child, living outside of the city, I had to discover my own pastimes if I wanted to do anything outside of my studies and chores. I remember in the heat of the summer, lying on the roof of our home, hoping for the smallest breezes to stir and bring relief. In the stillness, in the quiet of those long nights, I fell in love with the stars hanging over my head.

It was an old man who lived in the nearby village, not my father, who nurtured my interest. His was one home to which I brought the fresh masala dosas, idlis, and appams made by my mother. I would deliver them to his house last to have time to learn. He showed me the map of the stars and how to read their every movement. He told me of the prophecies of the ancients and how to watch for their advent in the skies. He taught me many things—languages, trade routes, and government. But it was the stars that captivated me. He saw that. Nurtured that. And before he died, he gave me his star charts, journals, and instruments. Gifts with which to track the ultimate gift.

I have spent my days searching manuscripts, traveling to gatherings of scholars, and waiting for the sun to set so I could read the news in the sky. Many of us feel that something will be revealed soon. The movement of the stars over the past months has been unusual. There is something we are meant to notice, meant to observe. I watch each night, adding notes to my charts with anticipation. I admit there has been some fear on my part. What if I fail in my endeavors? What if I miss the signs the heavens put on display? What if nothing happens in these next days and months at all?

I returned home last month from a gathering of great scholars from various regions. We met for days, watching the skies and sharing our wisdom. Two men agreed with what I understand to be imminent—Melchior from Persia and Balthazar from Babylon. Our observations were nearly identical. They inspired our understanding of the ancient prophets from the Hebrew scriptures and Syrian holy books. While we live in lands distant from one another, the stars have spoken to each of us similarly. We are confident a great sign is coming.

We anticipate traveling toward Jerusalem. Our interpretation of various religious texts directed our attention there. We have agreed to meet in Petra when the time comes. I know I can travel the trade routes of the Nabateans for the price of myrrh, which is easily obtained in my region. My distance from southern India is substantial, but I am prepared. All my life, I have been watching and waiting.

The sun is just setting now, and the stars are rising. I have been watching one that seems to increase in brightness. I am fascinated by it and think it could be what I have longed to see. I have my bags packed, charts rolled up, and instruments secured. I am ready. The darkness increases, and with it, I see my star. It is bigger and brighter than any other. It is unusual, unexplainable. And it hangs in the sky in the direction of Jerusalem. I am shaking with what this means. I stare a few moments more, and it only seems to glow bigger and brighter. This must be the sign I have longed to see in the skies I know so well. It tells me it's time to go now—in search of a promised King.

Section 2: THE WAY

The scroll of Isaiah the prophet was handed to him. He unrolled the scroll and found the place where this was written:

"The Spirit of the Lord is upon me,
for he has anointed me to bring the Good News to the poor.
He has sent me to proclaim that captives will be released,
that the blind will see,
that the oppressed will be set free,
and that the time of the Lord's favor has come."

He rolled up the scroll, handed it back to the attendant, and sat down. All eyes in the synagogue looked at him intently. Then he began to speak to them, "The Scripture you've just heard has been fulfilled this very day!"
Luke 4:17-21

7

SHE SPOKE

- ANNA -

Luke 2:22-40

THERE IS MORE COMMOTION on the temple grounds today. I have emerged from the Court of Women and look out across the Kidron Valley. Rubbing my back, I squint in the sun's brightness and feel every one of my years with the aches and pains of my body. I turn from the view of the valley and walk toward the Court of the Gentiles.

Activity surrounds me as people come and go; the temple life is vibrant. While I have a home in the city, I spend most of my waking hours here, praying and fasting. God speaks to me here. Sometimes the messages are for the priests and other religious leaders. More often, they are for the pilgrims who arrive from faraway places. He often tells me to speak words of hope over them. He directs my prayers for their needs, sometimes even for their healing.

I look out across the Court of the Gentiles and watch pilgrims of all kinds stop to exchange their Roman coins for Jewish currency. Then they will buy the animals needed to make the appropriate offerings in the temple.

I've watched this scene many times through the years, the desperation of the poor and alongside the confidence of the wealthy. The young and the old mix with locals and foreigners. It is quite a scene. Occasionally, my path would cross with someone, and I would know it was a divine encounter.

Today feels like one of those divine encounter kind of days. I survey the crowd, waiting for God to show me where to go. And then I see them. A husband and his wife, a small child in her arms. They have arrived in a caravan of others, dusty from travel, looking weary from a life on the road. Yet they smile at each other and the baby, and suddenly I hear the voice of the Lord telling me that I am seeing no ordinary babe. He opens my understanding, and I know I am now part of a holy moment, about to intersect with the divine in the flesh. The word "Messiah" moves past my ears like a light wind that promises something more.

I advance in their direction, but Simeon arrives first. A fellow servant of the Lord, Simeon devotes his time to God here in the temple courts, as I do. Together we have anticipated the coming of a Savior and longed to see it in our lifetimes. He receives the child from the mother's arms as he speaks to them. A small crowd is gathering. His voice fades in the wind before reaching my ears. But I don't have to hear him to know what he is saying or who he is holding.

As I reach the edge of the circle, I can see the tears on Simeon's cheeks and the wonder on the faces of these young parents. This is a moment like none other. I can hear a godly language that I am sure is meant only for me. I let it come because I know God is speaking. And I understand what he is saying. As I look at the child in Simeon's arms, I know I am actually looking at the face of God in the flesh. I hear his parents say his name—Jesus—the One who saves. And with that, I step into the circle where everyone turns to me out of reverence, and I begin to speak the words of God.

8

SUMMONED BY PARANOIA

- ELEAZAR -

Matthew 2:1-6

I THINK MY SISTER is right. Her husband is paranoid. Over the past few years, I have watched his erratic behavior, favoring those who pander to his wishes, striking out at those who don't, and changing his mind on opinions, not facts. Oh, don't get me wrong. Herod is a great man, an able king. What he has done for Jerusalem through the years is astounding. Just rebuilding the temple was a magnificent feat. Through that act alone, he has endeared many Jewish leaders to his reign, myself included. Yet, he is no exemplar of Jewish piety. He wades too far into pagan customs, watering down his Jewish upbringing. Herod offends the Pharisees and Sadducees, despite restoring their glorious temple.

But recent days have seen a darkening of his mood. His anger burns, no matter what is happening. My sister Mariamne tells me she is frightened of him. I, too, am concerned. And I am not naïve to think that either of my titles, High Priest or brother-in-law, will carry much weight with him if put to the test. So I, like many others around him, keep my head down. I go about my business in the temple, hoping he will stay in his palace and not look in my direction. Rumor has it that he has already killed three of his own sons. I want to keep my position of power.

I get up from the table where I have been studying the Torah for the past four hours. My eyes are weary, and my back is stiff. Crossing to the window, I look out over the city of Jerusalem. Even in the waning hours of the day, there is much activity. Pilgrims are always arriving or leaving through the city gates. Many of them come to the temple to present requisite sacrifices for events in their lives. I am glad their devotion to God motivates their honoring of him...and safeguards my lifestyle. I worked hard to be where I am. And I plan to stay here, High Priest of the Temple, for many years, whatever that takes.

The last of the sun dips below the horizon. The stars begin to rise, and among them is a star that burns brighter than the others. I have asked the royal astrologers about it, but they don't have a good explanation. Its appearance has me going back to the scriptures, reading and re-reading the prophecies I long ago ceased to believe. We have waited too long for the Messiah. God has no intention of saving us. Even so, the words of the prophet Micah stick in my mind, "But you, Bethlehem Ephrathah, though you are small among the clans of Judah, out of you will come for me one who will be ruler over Israel..." My eyes sweep toward the south as I ponder Bethlehem's possibility and improbability. This is a prophecy that could threaten many, including me. I am more aware than ever that my fate is tied to Herod's.

I turn back to the table and realize the summons from King Herod sits unanswered, and I remember his messenger standing just outside my door. Apparently, foreigners—magi—have arrived from eastern countries and are asking about the one born "King of the Jews." An ominous occurrence. To say the inquiry rattled Herod is a gross understatement. His fear will intensify below the surface until it erupts...likely in some kind of destruction.

I do not want to answer the summons, but I know refusing a king is not within my power. I slowly roll the manuscript with the prophecy about Bethlehem and walk toward the door. In the back of my mind, I wonder what could save me from Herod's paranoia. Will it be our kinship? Will it be how his power over Jerusalem intersects with my power over the temple courts? Our positions are mutually beneficial, to be sure. Will it be giving him a target for his fear?

As I walk toward the door, I am not assured, and I am no fool. I know my place in life is precarious right now, so I will tread lightly. I hope to tell Herod what he wants to hear. Yes, I am sure no "King of the Jews" is coming, but I will give Herod the city of Bethlehem, nonetheless.

9

UNDER THE FIG TREE

- NATHANAEL -

John 1:45-51 | Zechariah 3:8-10

HE SAW ME SITTING under the fig tree. It has been two days since my first conversation with him, and I still cannot get my head around that. How? Philip was the only one to see me there, to actually see me. He came to me that day and interrupted my studies with his enthusiastic, "We have found the very person Moses and the prophets wrote about!" I was studying the Torah intensely when he arrived and struggled to come out of the scriptures in which I had so profoundly embedded myself. Philip just kept talking. I could hear his voice, but I wasn't processing what he was saying until I heard him say, "His name is Jesus, the son of Joseph from Nazareth."

My head snapped up. "Nazareth! Can anything good come from Nazareth?" There was disdain in my voice; I know it. Such a small, un-remarkable village. I would not have known of it if not for having passed through it on my way from Cana to Nain several years back. Nazareth was nothing to note then...or now. How could Philip be saying that the Messiah might come from there? My mind spun. And then some details slowly took shape.

Philip was still chattering, but I turned my attention back to the Torah in my lap, a scroll borrowed for study and opened to the prophet Zechariah. The words I had just been reading jumped out at me as if God himself were speaking, "Soon I am going to bring my servant, the Branch." The branch. In Hebrew, the word for branch is *netzer*. Then I realized that the very name of that nothing village, Nazareth, is also rooted in *netzer*. And like that, it captivated me. Could it be? THE Messiah? Only minutes away from where I sat? The skeptic in me rose, not wanting to believe what I thought God was telling me. Philip's words break into my thoughts, "Come and see for yourself"

So I agreed. I wanted to see for myself. Perhaps an encounter with this Jesus from Nazareth could either dispel or confirm the thoughts screaming in my head: "The Branch, the Branch! The man from Nazareth, the Nazarene, is the one I have been reading about in the prophet Zechariah's own words!" I said nothing to Philip. I didn't want to be wrong. I didn't want to look stupid. I am a serious scholar. I built my life around studying the Torah and walking in its ways. Suddenly agreeing with this notion of the Messiah in the flesh had a touch of folly that I couldn't own.

Philip was impatient as I gathered my belongings quickly...but not too fast. I didn't want to seem overeager. I rolled the scroll up, carefully placed it in my bag, then slung it over my shoulder. I gestured to Philip to lead the way and took one tentative step after another as I slowly matched my pace to his. With each step, the craziness of the moment magnified. I felt this might just be the dumbest thing I have done since Philip and I were kids running through the streets of Cana. Despite the mocking voices in my head, I found my eyes straining to see what was in the distance as we walked. I craved that first sight of him. I was sure it would be all I needed.

I was feeling impatient for this encounter and then suddenly I saw them. A group of five men gathered in the distance. As we got closer, I immediately knew which one was the Nazarene. While the other four looked deep in conversation, the Nazarene's eyes found mine and did not leave. My steps faltered because there was a familiarity in his gaze that startled me. The distance between us dwindled quickly, and then there we were. Part of his group. There was a panicky feeling inside me and I couldn't look away from his face. He spoke to all of us, but really, his words were for me. "Now here is a genuine son of Israel—a man of complete integrity." He described my character as if we had known each other forever.

My mind scrambled for a response. I wanted to challenge him somehow, just to see what he would do. But all that tumbled out of my mouth was a simple, barely audible question that betrayed my wonder. "How do you know about me?" The silence in the air hung just a moment longer than was comfortable. Then he smiled and said, "I could see you under the fig tree before Philip found you."

My knees went weak as the words of Zechariah that I had only moments before committed to memory flooded my head: "Soon I am going to bring my servant, the Branch...each of you will invite your neighbor to sit with you peacefully under your own grapevine and fig tree." I didn't need anything else. I knew for sure this man, this Jesus from Nazareth, was the same Branch prophesied by Zechariah. I continued to stare into his face and take in the warmth of his smile. He knew I understood, that I had put together the play on words.

Netzer...Branch.

Netzer...Nazareth.

Jesus the Nazarene...the Branch from Nazareth.

Amazing.

I stood for a moment, speechless. Then, forgetting that we were in the company of others, I blurted out, "Rabbi, you are the Son of God—the King of Israel!"

He chuckled, "Do you believe this just because I told you I had seen you under the fig tree? You will see greater things than this."

Greater things. As I sit in a courtyard, awaiting a wedding feast in Cana, I again feel skeptical. What could be greater than a personal encounter with the one I know to be the Messiah, the Branch? I am part of his group now, his followers. We have left our homes, our employment behind to follow this Master, to learn from him. For me, it is enough just to be in his presence. Whatever he wants to teach, I will gladly know. The heart of this student is ready. It is not possible that there could be anything more significant.

10

WINE FOR A WEDDING

- MARY, THE MOTHER OF JESUS -

John 2:1-11

"WHAT DO YOU MEAN there is no more wine?" I gasp as I look into the panicked face of my best friend, the groom's mother.

"The servants just notified me. I had no idea." Her voice is higher than usual and beginning to shake. "We were so careful with the calculations. My husband, he reviewed my math and we thought it would be plenty." Her voice trails off, and I can see tears gather in her eyes. She is frantic. She knows, as do I, what this will mean for her family and their standing in Cana. It will shame and embarrass them. They will be socially ostracized for such an infraction. To run out of wine on the first night of wedding festivities? Utterly unthinkable. Yet here we are.

My mind is racing for solutions. We live too far away to get wine from home. Our wine is not nearly as good as what is being served here. The next option does not seem better. My eyes sweep the crowd for sympathetic friends who live here. Surely someone might have stores of wine we could use and then replace?

Next, my eyes come across the group of students my son has gathered. Unexpected guests to this wedding celebration. Unaccounted for on the guest list. But they are not the problem. They cannot have had such an impact on the wine. Their calm conversation tells me they have not over consumed. Perhaps I could send one or two of them on an errand. But where could they possibly acquire wine at this time of night? Nowhere. That is the truth. My friend's panic is starting to sink into my heart as well. Then my eyes rest on my son, and I catch my breath. Immediately, I know he is the solution.

I turn to my friend and try to reassure her with a smile. "Do not be anxious. I have an idea that I think could work." She looks so helpless through her unshed tears. I can see that she wants to believe me. I wish she knew what I did. About my son, that is. To everyone at this gathering, he is a carpenter's son who has left that trade to pursue a gift in teaching. He has gained recognition as an excellent teacher. My memories conjure up a picture of him as a boy, teaching in the temple in Jerusalem when he should have been heading home in a caravan with us. The panic of that day, of not being able to find him and thinking him missing...perhaps lost forever...resonates with the alarm my friend endures at this very moment.

But Jesus can change things. While he learned carpentry from his father Joseph, I know his ability to teach, to open the scriptures in ways that others cannot, is a gift from his other Father. Joseph is gone now, but the Heavenly Father is always nearby. He is near tonight. It is that relation-ship...Jesus and the Father...that can do the unthinkable. I just have to convince Jesus that now is as good a time as any. I am hopeful. Every hair on my arms is standing up. This is the moment that I have been waiting for. That the world should finally know Jesus as I do...

I quickly hug my friend and encourage her to join the dancing, though I know the last thing she feels like doing is dancing. I turn and weave through the crowd toward my son. The air feels alive to me, and I hurry. He sees me coming, and I can read in his face a curiosity. I beckon him away from his friends, and when he is next to me, I say, my voice full of expectation, "They have no more wine." A look of surprise flits across his face before he masters it and says in return, "Dear woman, that's not our problem."

He is right, of course. It really is not our problem to fix. Except that it is. Miriam is my longest and best friend. She is family in almost every way. I stare into his face, my eyes pleading, willing him to see my unspoken request. My mouth forms the word "please," though no sound comes out. His face softens slightly. I know at this moment what I am asking. The magnitude is not lost on either of us. He whispers, "My time has not yet come." Words I have heard many times over the past two years, and I backed down each and every time. Allowing him to discern when the time to embrace his full role was at hand.

But this time, I do not budge. I reach for his hand and hold it to my cheek. It's an intimate moment that recalls all the times through his childhood when he would touch my face and say, "I love you, Eema." I am watching his battle. It is part of this world and part of another. In this very moment, I can sense Heaven colliding with Earth. There is a swirl of emotion in his eyes, and I instinctively know he is struggling to honor God and me. His full humanity is at war with his full divinity. I wait. And I pray. I draw strength from the assurance I feel right now that the timing is right. I am just waiting for him to arrive at the same place. And then it comes. The warmth floods his eyes, and I squeeze his hand. He nods and falls into pace with me as I walk back toward the room where the wine had been stored.

We cross paths with some servants mid-way to our destination. They look distraught. The same panic is gripping them that I had seen in my friend. They do not know what I do. But very soon, they will. Very soon, many will know what I have always known. We are in the presence of the Messiah. The long-awaited One who will set God's people free. Everything is about to change. In the next moments, Heaven will lean into Earth, and nothing will be the same. I take a quick glance over my shoulder at my son, then turn to the servants and say, "Do whatever he tells you."

11

LIVING WATER

- SAMARITAN WOMAN -

John 4:1-44

I'M TRYING TO FIND the motivation to get up. But it escapes me, and I stay curled on the mat in the tiny, rundown excuse for a home that I have. I should go to the well now and get some water. I know the jar is empty, and from the heat surrounding me, I know the sun is high in the sky. It's long past the time when the other women would be at the well.

There was a time I would have joined them, a time when I was one of them. Young. Beautiful. Full of hope for the future. It seems so long ago. Five failed relationships ago, to be exact. My mother warned me. But I was in love and didn't care to wait for the traditions and blessings that would have meant a good, stable marriage for me. I stepped into life with the first man who promised love. I didn't listen to those who truly loved me.

When that relationship ended in failure, my place with the other women in the village ended, too. I became an outcast. From them, from my family. Divorced, I ceased to be welcome. Desperate, I looked for someone who could give me what I couldn't give myself...protection, a place to live, a name...value. But five marriages later, I lay on this mat in my tiny home with nothing but silence, poverty, and shame.

I can feel the tears begin to swim in my eyes, so I shake my head and propel myself off the mat. Reaching for the chipped, cracked clay jar, I steel myself for the daily journey to the village well in the heat of the sun and the stares of those who refuse to include me. I will move like a ghost through the dirt streets, and people's eyes will follow yet stare through me simultaneously. I hate it. I can't explain what it feels like.

I emerge from my hut into the full sun and my skin instantly responds to the warmth as moisture breaks the surface of my skin. With a quick wipe of my brow, I lift the clay pot to my head and begin the walk to the well. The only comfort I hold on to is that no one will be at the well at this time of day.

My feet shuffle in the dirt. I'm not in a hurry. With no one to interrupt my day, I have more time than I could want. But as I draw close to the well, my breath catches in my throat. Someone is sitting there. From what I can see, it is a man. A Jewish man. I stop in my tracks, not sure if I should continue. I have no business being in public alone. I do not have the protection of the other women in the village or a husband. It's not proper for me to go to the well if another man is there. My shoulders slump. I want to cry. All I want is some water and to go home.

I gather some courage and decide that I can just walk up to the well unnoticed, draw my water, and leave. If I don't look at him or talk to him, then maybe he will do what everyone else in my life does…ignore that I exist. I steer my footsteps to the side of the well where he is not sitting. I refuse to look in his direction as I arrive, though I can tell he is watching me. Lowering the jar from my head, I set it on the wall of the well as I reach for the rope I can use to lower it to the water. Sweat is trickling down my back, and my hands tremble. Please don't talk to me.

But then he speaks, "Please give me a drink."

My mind explodes in multiple directions at the same time and I can feel my heart pounding in my chest. He spoke to me. He acknowledged me. He asked for something from me. He waits for my response. He's a JEWISH MAN! This can't be happening. I have not looked at him yet. I'm not sure if I try to speak anything will actually come out. I am an outcast, Samaritan woman. I have no right to speak to this man. I draw a breath and finally say the last thought lingering in my mind.

"You are a Jew, and I am a Samaritan woman. Why are you asking me for a drink?"

His response is unexpected and curious. "If you only knew the gift God has for you and who you are speaking to, you would ask me, and I would give you living water."

Still looking away from him out of fear and respect, I want to understand. I say, "But sir, you don't have a rope or a bucket and the well is very deep. Where would you get this living water?"

His answer is lost on me because I can't stop shaking. He is talking to me. What will people say? Can my reputation sink any lower than it is? I grab onto this living water he offers because I feel as if, at any moment, I could die. "Please, sir, give me this water!" I say in barely a whisper, with tears forming in my eyes. "Then I'll never be thirsty again, and I won't have to come here to get water."

I wasn't prepared for his next request. "Go and get your husband."

A slight sound of despair escapes my lips. Tears drop on the ground as my legs become too weak to stand. I sink to my knees, and with a trembling voice, I admit to this stranger, "I don't have a husband."

He could shame me. He could yell at me to leave his presence. No one would stop him because my lack of status in this village would deserve it. I have no value and no one to care. But I only hear compassion in his strong, steady voice instead of harshness.

"You're right! You don't have a husband - for you have had five husbands, and you aren't even married to the main you're living with now. You certainly spoke the truth!"

He must be a prophet as there is no way he, a foreigner, a Jew, a passer-by at this well, could know the truth about me. Yet, he knows, and it doesn't stop him from talking to me. I hear him say, "You Samaritans worship what you do not know; we worship what we know, for salvation is from the Jews."

A teaching from what seems like a distant past creeps into my mind as I listen to him speak. Salvation. A savior. I heard something about that when I was a girl. Stories that my uncle used to tell me. Without thinking, I raise my eyes from the dirt to look at this man and find he is looking intently, patiently, and lovingly at me. I am startled. I feel like another human being sees me for the first time in years. The warmth of his expression washes over me, and I find I want to tell him what I know. I whisper, "I know the Messiah is coming - the one who is called Christ. When he comes, h—e will explain everything to us."

A smile spreads slowly across his face. I'm drawn in as he looks at me in the way I imagine a father would if I had one. The light catches his eyes, and he leans toward me as if to share a secret. "I AM the Messiah!"

12

A SON HEALED

- GOVERNMENT OFFICIAL -

John 4:46-54

I SIT IN THE last moments as the sun sinks over the horizon, watching my son's chest, still speechless. Only hours ago, his body was seized with a fever, writhing in pain, soaked in sweat, teetering on the edge of life. We tried so many things to make him well. The doctor had given up and left, shaking his head and silently communicating his sorrow.

Hours passed so slowly. The demands of everyday life faded in the face of my son's declining health. Friends stopped by to offer support. I know I talked to them, but I cannot recall one conversation. At one point, I remember feeling overwhelmed by the number of people in my house, and I told one of my servants to send them all home. I watched from a distance as our friends left. I heard the murmurs of surprise, some of them expressing feelings of hurt. In passing, someone mentioned Jesus of Nazareth being back in town. He wondered if Jesus could heal the boy.

A small flame of hope flickered inside my chest. What if he could? Everyone in town knew the stories. The water he turned into wine. The miraculous signs he displayed in Jerusalem. I shook my head. It wasn't sensible. Even if he could, why would Jesus care to heal my son? I serve in Herod's court. There is nothing about me that Jesus would like. But what if he could? What if he could heal my son?

Something inside me shifted. I hurried to grab a bag of supplies for the road, silently arguing with myself. Simultaneously believing that Jesus was the solution and that he was no solution.

I told the servants I was going to Cana and would be gone for two days. I asked them to send word if my son's condition worsened. They seem surprised that I was leaving. To be honest, it surprised me I was leaving. But there was something compelling about the peaceful feeling I got when I heard Jesus' name. I hurried out the door before they could ask any questions.

The journey, typically two days on foot, I accomplished in just six hours on horseback. It didn't take long to locate Jesus once I got to Cana. The crowd that followed him gave him away. I gathered my courage as I dismounted from my horse and tethered him to a nearby pole. What would I say? How could I possibly make my request in a way that he would pay attention to me? My courage faltered. I'm a fool. This is a fool's errand. But what if he could? I looked down the dirt road to where Jesus sat teaching, and my feet started to walk.

I tried to blend into the crowd, but my clothes gave my station away, and people stepped aside, making a clear path to Jesus himself. I stumbled forward, words tumbling from my mouth before I could think about them. I heard myself ask the initial question, the one in my head the whole way here. I asked him if he could heal my son. He stopped speaking and looked at me. I repeated my request, desperation creeping into my voice. I added he was close to death. He watched me with a steady gaze, and I felt seen in a way I never had before. I asked one more time if he could heal my dying son. Then he looked away from me and over the gathered crowd. After a moment, he spoke:

"Will you never believe in me unless you see miraculous signs and wonders?"

I wanted to believe. "Lord, please come now before my little boy dies," I whispered.

He looked back at me with the same steady gaze and the same sense of calm; this time, I saw compassion in his eyes. "Go back home," Jesus replied, "your son will live!" I knew in that instant what he said was true. His words were enough. I didn't need any other proof. With a tentative smile, I turned and walked to my horse. It was too late to journey home, so I found a room for the night.

The next day, I was halfway home when I encountered servants from my household. My heart stopped in my chest, not knowing what they would say, but hoping it was news I wanted to hear. With excitement, they told me my son was better. Somehow, I already knew that. And I knew why he was better. But I asked anyway. I asked them when my son's health improved. They said, "Yesterday afternoon at one o'clock his fever suddenly disappeared!"

Watching him sleep peacefully now, I hold on to what I know. Jesus healed my son. From a distance. With only words. And I believed every word he said. The confirmation came later when I spoke to my servants along the road. As they shared the moment my son's fever broke, I knew it was the exact moment I was with Jesus, hearing him speak life over my son. I believed his words, and I believe in him. The news spreading north from Sychar in Samaria is that Jesus is the Messiah. With all my heart, I believe that to be true.

13

Faith of a Friend

Mark 2:1-12 | Luke 5:17-26

"I DON'T THINK THIS is a good idea," I plead, voice wavering. My heart is pounding, anxiety rising.

"Of course, it's a good idea! Don't you want to be healed? I'm telling you, he can do that. I've seen him do it! A leper. I mean, A LEPER! You should have seen his skin, so full of weeping sores. The whole crowd recoiled when his path crossed ours. There was an instinctive retreat...everyone stepping back, longing to put more distance between ourselves and this unfortunate man. Except for him, for the Rabbi. He stepped CLOSER! He actually stepped toward a man with leprosy. I wish you could have been there, could have seen it! We held our breath collectively while the Rabbi told the man he was healed. 'Be healed!' He said it so simply, and just like that, the man's skin was clean. Not one sore in sight. Young, healthy, sun-kissed skin! I'm telling you, if he can do that by his words, this Rabbi can heal you, too."

The excitement in Eli's eyes is overwhelming to me. We have been friends since boyhood. He was one of the few kids who would talk to me, a cripple. He looked out for me then and is looking out for me now. I wish I could be excited like he is. But I can't. I just can't. Too many years of hoping and believing have left me skeptical that anything can change, and cynical that my body is worth healing. I likely would have completely

53

given up years ago, if not for Eli. And here he is now. So very excited. I wish I had just a glimmer of his faith. But I don't.

"Here they come!" he jumps up as he spies three men in the distance, walking toward us. "I told you they would come!"

Ben, Joash, and Simon. Friends of Eli's and, I guess, friends of mine. Though not really, I think. They are nice enough to me, but I think their kindness comes from their loyalty to Eli, not because they care so much about me. And who would? What good am I really? I can't walk, so I can't work. I never married. I'm not allowed in the synagogue. There is literally nothing of value I contribute to the world. Nothing to command someone's friendship or loyalty. I have no explanation for Eli. I don't know why he still bothers with me. I think he just gathers people to himself. I look at him now as he runs to meet his friends. I wish I could run. Run. Who am I kidding? I wish I could just feel my feet, my toes wiggle, and the itch of a blade of grass. Just something, anything, to let me know my legs work like they are supposed to.

"Okay!" Eli pants as he returns to my side. "They're ready. They think it's a great idea, too. See? I told you! Simon was with me when the Rabbi healed that leper. He saw what I saw. This Rabbi, he can help you; I know he can!"

Eli's friends are still standing in the distance, waiting. Eli's excitement seems to have been contagious. They are all smiling, too, and for one small second, I have some hope. But like a flame in the wind, it flickers out when I look down at my legs. In the face of such optimism, I am still defeated. "Eli," I whisper, then my voice catches in my throat as tears fill my eyes, and I look away so I don't have to see the immediate concern cloud over my friend's face. He kneels beside me, calmly, quietly, earnestly. He puts his hand on my shoulder as tears silently roll down my cheeks.

"Rafael, please. You can do this. *We* can do this. He will heal you. I just know he will. You have to try. You have to trust me. We will take you. We will be with you. Please."

"I'm so scared," my voice is barely audible. But he is close enough to hear and his hand squeezes my shoulder reassuringly.

"I know, my friend. But what if you could walk again? What if you could run like when we were kids, before the accident? What if? Isn't it worth the try?"

"Eli…" my voice trails off, and silence settles in for a minute. He waits. Patiently, steadfastly, he waits. "What if we try, and it doesn't work? What if he is too busy? What if this Rabbi has no time for this useless cripple?"

"Don't say that, Rafi. Don't. You have to believe."

"I'm not sure I can."

He looks intently at me. After a moment he says, more assured than ever, "Then I'll believe enough for the both of us!" He is smiling now, the glimmer of excitement beginning to take residence in his body again. Almost as if the weight of being serious for those few moments was too much for his buoyant soul. He turns and waves to the others to join us.

"Simon," he says, "tell him. Tell him what you saw. The man with leprosy. Tell Rafael what you saw."

Simon stands for a moment, looking at me, then at Eli, then back to me. "I'm sure he told you, but I will tell you again. We witnessed a miracle. I don't know how he did it, but that man healed a leper. Clean. Totally clean. As if he has never had an illness in his life. He has powers. Some are saying he is the Messiah."

Messiah. The word settles into my core, and something sparks. The smallest of flames sputters to life, and for the first time in what seems like forever, I feel the beginnings of hope. What if they are right? What if I can be healed? Yesterday I would have given anything to walk again. Why is it that now, when the possibility of that very thing is offered, I am gripped by such terror? I frown, and just like that, the fragile flame inside dwindles. Who am I kidding? If he is the Messiah, he will have no time for me. This is a bad idea. I look up at their faces and try to dismiss them by pointing out, "If he's the Messiah, there will be no getting close. Whatever room he is in will be packed with people. We won't even get close to the door."

Eli, not to be deterred a moment longer, as if his patience with me has finally run out, looks at me and, with deadly precision, says, "What does your name mean, Rafael?"

I'm confused. What does that have to do with anything at all? Then, like lighting a candle in a dark room, I can see. Before I can answer, comes Eli's voice, "That's right. 'God heals.' That is what your name means, and that is what he will do. If I have to tear a hole in a roof, God will heal you today."

14

Just One Touch

Mark 5:24-34 | Luke 8:42b-48

I CANNOT REMEMBER A day in recent years when I didn't feel highly fatigued for the better part of the day. It is an unwelcome sensation that greets me in the morning and sends me off to sleep at night. I count it a good day if I can get out of bed before noon. And stay out of bed until after dinner.

It wasn't always like this, of course. As a child, I did what other young girls did with their time. I had chores to do and skills to learn. And friends to play with when my responsibilities at home were done. We laughed, ran, danced, and dreamed together, but then I got sick. And no one could find a cure. My parents tried to hide it from others, but somehow the details got out, and the isolation began. One by one, friends stopped coming by. No one invited us for Shabbat dinners. We were not allowed to enter the synagogue. My dad's work as a handyman dried up. I was only twelve at the time.

Over the next two years, I watched horrified as my family became increasingly destitute. With little to no income and no community, my parents turned to the small parcel of land we had next to our house to grow their own food. Not welcome in the markets, my mother became adept at growing fruits and vegetables. We had some chickens that could lay eggs. Not much, but enough to survive. One day, my brother stole olives from a tree and brought them home. My mother made him return them to the man who owned the tree. I saw the tears in his eyes and the pain in hers as they walked out of our house together. That moment changed me. I decided I had to leave. For the sake of my family, I had to leave.

I waited a few days as I gathered an armful of belongings and hid them in a basket. Scarves for my head, to hide my face. A change of clothes and my cloak placed beside my bag of rags. Those cursed rags. A sign of the illness that weakened me every day and tore my family away from the fabric of society. The basket packed, I waited for the sun to set, for night to come, and sleep to overtake my family. Then I left, sorry for the pain I had caused and would continue to cause.

That was ten years ago. I had arrived in Capernaum with just two shekels, my basket, and all the courage I could summon. I kept to myself, living in an abandoned cave carved into a limestone wall at the city's edge. I grew my food like my mom had. Every so often, I hid my identity and illness so I could take a small job in town and save money. Then I would quit before anyone asked questions. My family never came looking for me. That was painful to process. No one to call me daughter anymore. Ultimately, I just chose to be happy for them, even though I was personally fractured.

The reality of today slowly reclaims my attention, and I remember what will get me out of bed. There is a new teacher in town. I heard people talking about him yesterday while waiting my turn to draw water from the well. They spoke of his wisdom, knowledge of the Torah, and ability to debate with religious leaders. But what they said next made my breath catch in my chest. They said he was a healer. That he had healed lepers and cripples and even people who had died! And he was here, in Capernaum. It seemed too good to be true. I waited for the women to leave, scooped up some water, and walked home as quickly as I could, thinking about the Healer the whole way.

That is what will get me out of bed today. The Healer. I heard he will teach in the city this afternoon and am determined to find him. It should be easy. I will just walk the streets, unseen like usual, listening to the chatter and watching for crowds. If he is as amazing as the women at the well said, others will also look for him. I plan to find him and when I do, I will ask him to heal me. I allow myself to think about that for a moment. What would that be like? After twelve years of bleeding, exhaustion, and exile, what would it be like to be healed? A small cry escapes my lips, the possibility too much to contain.

Clinging to that hope, I rise and wrap my head in a scarf, imagining it somehow contains the extra courage I will need. I compel my ice-cold feet to move forward and take my body with them. About five years into this illness, my hands and feet stopped feeling warm. I do not know why. I spent most of my savings to pay for cures from various doctors. But nothing worked. Nothing at all. I live with a constant mix of desperation and defeat. That thought motivates me to keep walking.

I see a crowd has gathered at the intersection of the city streets ahead, and I panic. What am I doing? Why did I think this could work? Who am I to join a crowd where my unclean state could infect others? What if I am recognized as the sick woman who lives on the edge of town? Then I see him. It has to be him. He looks like a teacher, wearing the clothes of a rabbi, complete with the tasseled robe. The crowd swirls around him and I am drawn forward. There is a strange sense of being compelled against my will. The closer I get, the more my fears rise and my courage flees. I do not think I can do this. In fact, I know I cannot. I can't talk to him, ask for healing. I've come so far, but...

Then I have an idea. If he really is a powerful healer...one who can restore the dead...maybe it would be enough if I just touch his robe? I could do it from behind. In the crowd he would never know, would he? I mean, how could he? I find I am suddenly laser focused. This is it. Either it works or it doesn't, but I have to try. I insert myself into the crowd and press forward.

He is walking quickly, which is hard for me. But his robe flows behind him in the breeze, and I surge forward, my fingertips barely brushing one tassel. I stumble, catch myself, and stop in my tracks, squeezing my eyes shut as I marvel at the warmth traveling through my body. I am speechless and unable to explain what is happening to me. I assume the Healer will continue to travel forward with the surrounding crowd, and as I open my eyes I am surprised to find he has also stopped walking. Then I hear these words, "Who touched my robe?"

I stand rooted to my spot, terrified. He knows. I want to run in the other direction. What was I thinking? But my body continues to warm, and I know that I have been healed by the smallest of touches. He is every bit the Healer people have called him. Emboldened by what I know has transpired, I have just enough courage to step out of the crowd. But then I fall, trembling, on my knees before him.

My confession comes quickly. I tell him what I have done, that I was the one who touched his robe, uninvited. That I was desperate to be healed after twelve tortuous years. That I heard he could heal, and that I dared to believe. Then I hold my breath and wait for what is likely to be public humiliation, possible rage. I remember that I am unclean... which means he is now, too. But then I hear him speak a word I have not heard in a long time, "Daughter."

I begin to sob, something breaking loose in me that I did not even realize I had walled up so long ago. I feel the gentle touch of his hand on my shoulder and cannot help it when I flinch. No one has voluntarily touched me in years. I glance up at him and see his smile as he adds, "Your faith has made you well. Go in peace. Your suffering is over."

15

IN THE BALANCE

- JAIRUS' DAUGHTER -

Luke 8:40-42a,49-56

I CAN HEAR ALL around me. People coming and going. I hear my mother crying. I hear my father bark orders at our servants. My mother's hand squeezes mine as her tears splash warmly on my skin. A cold cloth is on my head, gently laid there only minutes ago. I hear whispers about me that are laced with the fear that I am dying. I'm not. I'm not dying. But I can't tell them that.

There is something terribly wrong with me. I cannot open my eyes. I cannot speak. In truth, I cannot move any part of my body except to breathe and swallow the broth they spoon into my mouth. I feel incredibly warm, but I can't tell them to take the covers off, so I stay tucked into my bed, wishing for a cool breeze to float through the window. No one knows what is wrong.

At my latest count, my father has paid for three different physicians to see me. One by one, they cautiously entered my room. I hear the hesitancy in their voices, the unspoken fear that whatever is wrong with me could be given to them. My father has had to remind them they are being paid for their services. But they have no answers. All of them have said it is only by the grace of God that I am still breathing. They seem to think that I will leave soon. But I have no intention of leaving. I am very much alive!

Today there is a new energy in the house. While kept in a side room, I can still hear what happens in the main living area. Someone is preparing for a journey. I have listened as servants prepare food and discuss details about which animal to ride or if walking might be better. My father's voice is in the mix, so I assume he is the one who is leaving. I'm just not sure where he is going or why. Perhaps it is a matter of business. He is an important man, a ruler in the synagogue. But he has not left the house for days. He has spent most of his time praying for a miracle in my room.

I see shadows pass by my bed, interrupting the sunlight from the window. Someone is approaching to speak to my mother, who still holds my hand, though her tears have stopped. They whisper as if talking might disturb me. I can hear every word and I find I am right. My father is the one leaving the house. He is going to look for a traveling healer named Jesus. He is convinced that Jesus can save me. He walked to the neighboring village in search of this man.

We have all heard rumors about Jesus. He has been in and around Galilee for quite some time, his companions a group of twelve students. He is called Rabbi because he teaches about God in the synagogue and out in the fields, in boats, at weddings, and on hillsides. They say he spends time with people from all walks of life. But the stories of his healings spread the quickest and leave all of us wondering at his power. Some have whispered the name "Messiah" to describe him. From what I have heard, I would not be surprised. This is the man my father is going to find.

As I ponder that, I realize my situation must seem very desperate if my father, a synagogue leader, is going in search of Jesus. The talk over the past weeks has been that the synagogue leaders distrust Jesus. They refuse to consider that God might have sent him. According to my father, they have rejected that idea. He thinks that is closed-minded and foolish. He believes they should pay attention.

These are the discussions I have overheard as I lay on my bed, unable to move or tell the world I am still here. I used to be able to squeeze my fingers around something and to move the muscles in my face to squeeze my eyes tight. Now I find I cannot move anything. I cannot even seem to swallow the broth anymore. People are scared. They say it is a sign I am dying. My mother is distraught. I think this is why my dad is going to find Jesus. I long to tell them I am still here. It is the last thought in my mind as I drift to sleep and the mournful sounds of those in the room fade away.

———————·———————

"My child, get up!" The voice that wakes me is intense, confident, and warm. I open my eyes and sit up, forgetting where I have been these past weeks, that my life was hanging in the balance. I see the man who has just spoken, his kind eyes connecting with my heart as warmth spreads from my chest throughout my body. Just past him, I see three men whose faces register both surprise and joy. But it's when I turn my head toward my father's voice and see his face, and that of my mother's, that the gravity of the moment settles in.

I have been restored from the darkness of death to the light of the living by the man with kind eyes and a warm voice. This is Jesus. My father found him, and I am saved.

16

IN THE SHADOWS

- ANDREW -

Matthew 14:22-33

I CAN'T PUT INTO words the searing pain racing through my arms and back. I have been pulling at these oars for hours and we are no further than the middle of the lake. We should have long ago reached the opposite shore. Honestly, there are twelve of us in this boat. Strong men. Men used to hard work. We have been rowing too long. As one reaches his limits, another steps in. Our progress has been maddeningly slow. It's the wind. Slamming against us no matter how much strength we put behind each stroke.

I knew we shouldn't have gotten in the boat. We should have stayed with Jesus, but he made us go. He insisted we leave him behind. I have no idea how he will meet up with us. It will be a tremendously long walk...he has no donkey. He has no boat of his own and certainly could not row it against this wind...one man would be overcome by this wind. Well, after what I saw today, perhaps Jesus could defy even the wind.

I shake my head to refocus on my task. My hands are raw from the wood and my strength is waning. Just when I think I can't raise the oar for another pull, my brother steps in and takes the oar from me. Peter. He is here because of me. I told him about Jesus. I told him. But here I sit in his shadow. Peter is always at the front, always the one grabbing the attention. This has been the truth of my life lived with Peter.

I slump to the floor near the back of the boat, my breathing ragged as the spray from the waves coats my face. Typically, being out on the water is a comfort to me. As a fisherman by trade, I've lived more of my life in a boat than out. But tonight I am spent and I don't want to be here. I'm wet and cold and sore and annoyed.

I think back to earlier in the day when the sun was still shining, and we were trying to go with Jesus to a quiet place. As usual, people found and gathered around him...even in the desolate location we had picked. People everywhere. Always people. Like a fisherman casts a net and hauls fish into his boat, Jesus hauls in people. It's one of the ways we know he is not your average person. And we watch him respond to those people patiently (and sometimes not so patiently). Sick people, religious people, despised people. He receives them all. People who are polite, patient, and indifferent. People who are needy, greedy, and rude. People who are curious, kind, and thoughtful. Elders, scholars, working men...he even includes women and children. Extraordinary.

I have not processed the events of earlier today. Thousands had gathered to hear him teach and as evening approached, we advised him to send them home. We were not prepared to feed them. Small details to Jesus. He asked us how much food we had and waited for an answer. No one spoke.

We looked around to see what we could find. But it was after the time for the mid-day meal and everyone had long since eaten what they had brought. Even so, we walked through the crowd, calling for food. I found a boy who still had his lunch. As I looked in the sack, my pessimism took over. Five loaves of bread and two fish. It was comical. It was absurd. But I brought it to Jesus and showed him what we had. Then I waited for him to laugh at me. He should have laughed at me.

Instead, he fed everyone...EVERYONE. Thousands of men, women, and children. Fed them all. Every single person got a small feast. Not just a bite or a crumb, but more than enough to fill their stomachs and leave extras. We passed out this food. It took a long time. I did not say a word for hours. How did he do it? How could I hand out food, food and more food and not have an empty basket? It defied logic. It took my wonder about this man to mind-numbing levels. When he told us to get into the boat at the end of the day, I wanted to argue. I wanted to stay with him. I wanted to ask, "What did we just witness?" and have him explain it to me in a way I could understand. Instead, I got in the boat.

I am startled from my thoughts by screaming. My head snaps up and I see what is causing the trouble. Amid the whipping wind and the waves that crash into our boat, I see what appears to be someone on the water walking toward us. Impossible! I have never seen such a sight and as my mind grapples with yet another "too strange to be true" moment, I suddenly hear my brother call Jesus' name and then climb over the side of the boat. What is he doing?! He will surely die in these waves. I scramble to the boat's edge and yell "Peter!" as I grip the wood. Then I look beyond him and see he is right. It is Jesus. He really is there an he is talking to us. HE…IS…WALKING…ON…THE…WATER! And now my brother is, too. I can only stare. I cannot move.

With my heart in my throat, I watch my brother walk on the top of the waves toward Jesus. It is terrifying and marvelous at the same time. Then, suddenly, he is sinking. I lift my leg to jump into the water to save him and then realize I don't have to. Jesus has already done it. With just a touch of his hand…a grip on Peter's forearm…Peter is above the waves again and returning to the boat. They both get in. I still cannot move. I haven't even sorted out the fish and loaves thing, now this? This water walking moment steals my breath away. What is going on? How can this happen?

I can feel myself trembling as I sink to my knees. The others have gathered around Jesus and Peter. Their shouts and fear have moved through nervous laughter to warm embraces and I am left on the outside, still in the shadow. Of course, it would be Peter who walked on water. It's always Peter. I stare at the bottom of the boat.

I'm unsure how much time has passed, but I realize the boat is no longer pitching sharply. There is no more spray in my face. No one is at the oars. The wind is still. I look up and find I am looking into the eyes of Jesus watching me. He sees me. Peter is still beside him, still talking, but he sees me. He sees past my uncertainty, past my fear, past my skepticism. He says my name...Andrew...and suddenly I am reminded who fed those people on the hillside today. I know who can walk on water and calm the wind. I know who sees me as I am and loves me...all of me. He is Jesus. He finds me in the shadows and pulls me into his light with just one look...one mention of my name. He is Jesus. My Messiah.

17

Stones Fall

John 8:1-11

I LIE HERE IN the early morning light, the rising sun just beginning to make its presence known. But I feel cold. I feel empty. It's always like this. Every morning I am disappointed as my eyes open and I find I am no different than I was yesterday. A shell of a woman with no value beyond the use of my body for someone else. The spot next to me is still warm, though its occupant has already risen and left for the day. I squeeze my eyes shut. I should not be here. I need to leave, but I don't know how. A tear traces a lonely path from the corner of my eye, down my cheek, and onto the sheets. I feel like nothing can motivate me to get up and leave this house.

Suddenly, there is a commotion outside and a pounding at the door. I can hear my husband's voice, among others, yelling for the door to be opened. I panic and sit up, reaching for a garment to wear. Then, without warning, seven men, my husband among them, crash into the room. The venom in his voice paralyzes me as he says, "I told you she would be here! Is there any question what she has done?" The others with him stare at me with condemnation, and I know there is nowhere I can go. I feel the coldness increase even though the day is warm. And I flinch at the pain in my arm as one of them grabs me, hauls me out of bed, and pushes me to the door. I glance at my husband as I pass, in time to see the disappointment on his face.

Very quickly, I am forced from the quiet and solitude of the house to the public eye of a busy morning street in Jerusalem. People stop and stare, some with mouths open, as I stumble, barely dressed, through the streets. Half pulled; half dragged...very much against my will. But I can say nothing. Do nothing. My sin is great, and I know it. The payment will be high. And I know that too. The columns of the Temple rise in the distance and I know I am headed for a very public judgment, one absent of compassion or mercy. Don't they see that as a woman I have no choice? In a world full of men, I have absolutely no choice.

We arrive in the Temple courtyard sooner than I could have imagined. My feet are cut and bleeding from the forced walk without sandals. But I am numb, and the pain barely registers. My angry accusers drag me over to a crowd of people who have gathered to hear someone teach. My head sinks forward, chin to my chest, overcome by shame, fear, and emptiness. I hear some talking, but just can't bear to raise my head to accept the presence of others. More than anything, I just want to be a little girl again, dancing in the summer sun.

"Teacher," one of them interrupts as I am shoved before him. "This woman was caught in the act of adultery. The law of Moses says to stone her. What do you say?" His voice is challenging, impatient, mocking. I am devoid of hope. This most certainly will not end well. I can feel my knees weaken and am worried that soon I will be unable to stand. But would that not be welcome? To crumple to the ground? A heap of miserable skin and bones? Indeed, no one would care about me then. There is little to indicate they care about me now. The silence hanging in the air as they await the teacher's answer is oppressive. It stretches on.

I continue to stare at the dirt mixing with the blood on my feet. I decide to focus on the little girl I conjured up moments earlier. Her joy, her laughter, her warmth. It's such a distance from where I am now. I will myself to go there and be her. To remember the days when I was her. I'm startled from my forced daydream by the sight of a finger drawing in the dirt near my feet. I stare at it. It becomes my new focal point to escape the present. I look through my disheveled, unbraided hair and see it is the teacher himself who has put off answering and instead, writes in the dirt. Such strange behavior! Why doesn't he tell them they are correct, seal my fate, and return to his teaching? The energy in this moment is rising and I suddenly notice several men holding stones, just waiting, silently begging the teacher to answer so they can let those stones fly.

And there it is. So abrupt. Without warning. My life's end is excruciatingly visible to me. Will it hurt? Will I even feel those stones when they strike? Do they have the power to make me feel worse than I already do? Or do they have the power to set me free? Like a wild animal that will chew off its own limb to survive. Will the pain that comes in the next minutes be the necessary path to a final place of release? I am terrified that I consider death to be more welcome than my life. There is an incredible pain in my chest that chokes a breath from me and unlocks the tears I have so desperately been holding back. But then he speaks. He slowly rises and simply says, "Let the one who has never sinned throw the first stone!"

I freeze. Every muscle tensed for what comes next. The coldness I have felt since morning grows deeper. The little girl in my mind has stopped dancing as if she, too, is cowering in fear. One thud breaks the strained silence and then another, followed by more thuds and the sound of feet shuffling away. I dare to take a look, amazed that the thud I first heard was not a stone colliding with my flesh. No. They were all stones hitting the ground as all of my accusers, my husband included, dropped their stones and walked away. I am stunned.

I turn back toward the teacher, and he has returned to writing in the dirt. I don't say anything. I have no words. I do not understand. What is he writing, anyway? I wish I could read. The dread and panic have not left, for I know this man still holds power over me. I cannot leave unless he bids me to go. My tears are still falling, and one splashes on the top of my foot. He stops writing, stands, and looks at me. By accident, my eyes meet his. I did not mean to. It would have been more proper for me to look away. But now, it's too late to look away.

His voice startles me when he asks, "Where are your accusers? Didn't even one of them condemn you?" His words are soft, his tone inviting. I am not sure what to do with that. No one has ever treated me with respect. But this man, this one, is focused only on me. Though there are others in the courtyard, I am the recipient of his full attention. I swallow and whisper, still looking into his eyes, "No, Lord." He smiles and I feel something break loose inside of me. Like something bound has suddenly been set free. It floods me from the top of my head down to my filthy toes.

"Neither do I." he says quietly, just to me. "Go and sin no more." I hold his gaze one second longer to be sure what he says is real. Then I slowly turn and walk away. He has shown mercy. He has bestowed compassion. He has saved my life. These truths are gradually sinking in. With each step, I realize I am more whole than ever. Worthy. Valued. His own eyes told me so. And I am filled with something else I have not felt in a very long time. Warmth. The cold emptiness that has been my forever companion is slowly being pushed away as this little girl begins to dance.

Section 3: A Long Goodbye

Jesus for me always clinches the deal, and I sometimes wonder why I did not listen to him in the first place.

Richard Rohr
Falling Upward: A Spirituality for the Two Halves of Life

18

A Whisper of More
Part 1

- SERVANT GIRL -

Mark 14:12-17 | John 13:1-17

I'm just a serving girl. At barely fourteen years of age, my life isn't worth much. I live with my parents and six siblings. Two brothers are older than me, but I'm the oldest girl. My parents have just started conversations with another family in our neighborhood that may lead to an eventual marriage for me. My life is simple. I have learned all the skills my mother taught me to be a good wife and mother. These things occupy my life most of the time. But as the Passover comes near and Jerusalem's population swells with the faithful coming to the city, I find my thoughts are consumed by the events I witnessed nearly one year ago. My memory returns to a band of men sharing a meal in an upper room...

A neighbor asked my mother to prepare a room and a Passover meal for some travelers coming into town. She brought me along to help her. The room was on the second level of the man's home, not far from ours. Together we gathered all that would be needed for the meal: the wine, the unleavened bread, the special herbs, and other symbolic foods and brought them to the house. There were two men there when we arrived. They seemed grateful to have our help in supplying the items needed for such an important meal. My mother kindly greeted them.

"Here is a simple room, but it will work for your meal. We have cleaned it, and in this basket, we have placed the items needed for your Passover celebration. You will find cushions for sitting over in that corner," she said as she pointed to the neatly stacked cushions across the room. "Is there anything else you require?" I stood quietly behind her, eyes focused on the floor.

"You have provided all that we asked, and we are grateful. Is there a pitcher and a towel we might use for washing?" one of them asked.

"Oh, yes. They are here by the door. I will send my daughter to draw water for you." She flicked her hand at me and I moved toward the door, reaching to pick up the pitcher on my way. I went down the stairs quickly and walked around the back of the building to the rain barrel to draw water with the pitcher. The sun was setting, but the city's noise had yet to fade. I turned quickly and took the stairs two at a time, not wishing to keep the men, or my mother, waiting.

As I entered the room, I overheard the men asking if one of us might stay through the meal in case something else was needed. I wanted my mom to be the one to stay. I winced slightly as I heard her volunteer me and assure the men that I was an obedient and capable serving girl. I sighed and poured the water from the pitcher into the basin, setting the empty pitcher beside it. I turned to look at my mother and waited for additional instructions. The men thanked her, and then they walked past me and out of the room.

My mother turned to me and smiled, "You will stay and help. I will send your brother over if you need someone stronger to accomplish a task. He will walk you home. Be sure to remember all I have taught you. Serve these men well. They are important. They are friends of the man named Jesus that your father has been talking about."

I bowed my head, "Yes, mother."

She put her hand on my cheek and walked past me to hurry home to prepare our meal for the Passover celebration. I stood with my back to the wall and looked around the room. It was quiet. It was ready. Thirteen places for people to sit. I looked at the empty pitcher, then scooped it up to go back and fill it for the meal. Down the stairs again, and as I walked out the door, I could see a band of men in the distance, heading in my direction. I slowed my walk and took my time, so they could arrive and settle in before I returned to the room. I heard them walk up the stairs to the room from the back of the building. They were not particularly noisy. Not like other groups of men I have passed in the city. Their voices faded inside. I waited a few more minutes before I picked up the pitcher and made my way to the front of the building and up the stairs.

As I neared the door, I could see that one of them had already grabbed the towel, tucked it into his waist, and was moving toward the others with the water basin. Embarrassed, I didn't go in. Servants are supposed to wash feet. Tonight, here in this room, I was supposed to wash their feet. I was mortified. Should I walk in? And if I did, would I even have the courage to say anything? It isn't a servant girl's place to address a room full of men. I was gripped with fear and lingered just outside the door, wishing I could enter and do it right, but knowing I would not. Time seemed to stand still, and all I could picture was the look of disappointment on my mother's face.

I am unsure how long I stood there, rooted to the floor by my fear. Voices from the men registered in my ears again as I heard one of them say with passion, "No. You will never, ever wash my feet." His voice was gruff and full of pride. A quieter, calmer voice that was no less strong responded, "Unless I wash you, you won't belong to me." It was enough to silence the first man and even though I was not watching, I could hear the water splashing and knew his feet were being cleansed, despite his protest. I felt horrible. If I had been where I was supposed to be, I would be washing their feet and I doubt anyone would have protested.

I was startled from my thoughts by the arrival on the stairs of my brother. He looked confused, seeing me outside the room with the water pitcher in my hands. He walked beside me and whispered, "What are you doing out here?"

"I went to draw water for the meal, but when I returned, the men were washing their own feet. I didn't know what to do!"

"So, you're hiding in the hallway?"

I shot him a look to state the obvious. He must have seen the fear in my eyes because he softened and nudged my shoulder, saying, "It'll be okay. Wait until the conversation picks up and you can slide in with the fresh water. They will not notice a serving girl like you."

He was right. The rest of the meal progressed. I got the courage to go inside and set the pitcher on the table. Then I stood off to the side, waiting to see if there would be anything else they needed from me. But they were deep in conversation, their voices rising and falling with excitement and confusion. I noticed the one with the towel seemed to be the leader. When I heard them call him "Lord," I realized he must be the Jesus my mother had mentioned. The embarrassment from the missed foot washing earlier in the evening was renewed. This Jesus, their lord, had been the one to wash their feet! Who does that? What lord washes the feet of others?

Those questions were barely formed in my mind when I noticed the men were standing up and getting ready to leave. I pressed myself against the wall in the room's shadows because I didn't want to be noticed. As they walked out, I kept my eyes on Jesus. There was just something about him. So calm. So steady. So focused. He did not have the nervous energy that the others had. They were just about out of the room when he turned and looked right at me and smiled. Then he left the room, taking all the energy with him. Without thinking, I followed.

19

DRINK OF THE CUP

- ANDREW -

Matthew 26:17-30 | Mark 14:12-26

WE HAVE HAD MANY meals with Jesus over the years, yet this one seems strangely different. He seems different. Something about his face, his eyes, seems thoughtful and heavy. From where I sit, I can see that something has shifted in him.

He's talking with John. My brother Peter is trying to listen in. Peter. I consider him for a moment. I have always known him to be larger than life. He is everything that I am not. He's loud. He's adventurous. He's confident. He's always in the center. Me? I'm the quiet one. Watching, waiting to see what people will do. For three years, I have simply soaked in everything I can about Jesus. But it's hard to take in Jesus and not also receive Peter.

Jesus walked on water...Peter did, too. Jesus went up on a mountain to meet with God...Peter tagged along. Jesus needed someone to set up this dinner tonight...he sent Peter. I guess I don't blame him. There is something really great about my brother. That thought automatically makes me think there is not much that is great about me. I cringe at the jealousy in me that rises up. The truth is, I am envious of Peter's relationship with Jesus. I just have to be honest about that.

And here, again, Peter has claimed center stage in this space. First, in his refusal to allow Jesus to wash his feet. I'll admit it was odd to have Jesus put a towel around his waist like a servant and wash the dirt and grime from my feet, carefully cleaning even between my toes. But unlike Peter's protest, I receive what Jesus is doing. I can't really name it or call it out, but I know it is crucial. And like so many other things, I know it will make sense later.

Then Peter was volunteering to follow Jesus wherever he goes...even if it means he might die. Peter's statement is big and brash. He doesn't get it. Jesus is actually going to die, and soon. He told us so himself. He mentions it, he hints at it, and he prays about it. I don't know the hour of his death, but I know it's imminent. I can feel it. I glance around the room at the faces of the other men. They seem distracted. Judas is missing, but I remember he left quickly after talking to Jesus about something.

The darkness is pressing in. Outside, the sun has set. In here, there is darkness, too. Lost in my thoughts, I have missed much of what Jesus was just saying, but I tune in just in time to hear him say, "Take it, for this is my body." He broke the bread in half and passed it around the circle, sharing it with us. Then he picked up the wine goblet and said, "This is my blood, which confirms the covenant between God and his people. It is poured out as a sacrifice for many."

He passed it around and as I tipped the cup to my lips, my eyes met those of Jesus and I knew this would be my last meal with him.

20

DISINTEGRATION

- JUDAS ISCARIOT -

John 13:21-30

I WISH IT WOULD stop. The voice. The one in my head that speaks lies that sound like truth. It began with my cynicism and self-doubt. Carefully curated over the past three years of traveling with eleven other men and with him, with Jesus. Everything he does is amazing. But everything I do is a disappointment. It has always been so.

I remember my childhood well. I believed I could do something good, something helpful, something useful. But then, well, I didn't. What I thought of myself in my head never materialized in the world. I always came up short. I always received someone's judgment. I thought I could do better, but I never actually did. Slowly, I realized no one thought I would amount to much. No one, that is, except my mother.

She encouraged. She loved. She accepted me. She believed I could be more. Then she died. So I stopped trying. It was easier to embrace my reality than to foster the hope that I could be more...only to find I wasn't. Without her presence, there was no one to believe in me.

Until he came into my life. There was so much about him that was like her. He never judged me, though I felt like I judged him all the time. He saw things in me. He accepted me as I was and breathed potential back into my life. At first, it was so foreign. Then, slowly, I remembered.

I remembered what it was like to feel seen, to feel valuable. He did that for me in the early days when we had just started traveling and no one knew who he was.

But that changed. And the way I saw him changed, too. It was harder to get his attention. There were so many others who took up his time. I tried to stay close to him, desperate to keep believing in the potential he saw in me. But more people pressed in and I allowed myself to move to the background. Once an eager part of the twelve, I believed the old voices in my head. And I doubted what he saw in me. I doubted I had the value he said I had. I stopped believing in myself and in him.

A new voice had come. And it's this voice that I wish I could silence. It's the voice of an enemy, I know it. I fight against it. But it seems like it's useless, and I know that, eventually, I will just succumb to it. I can feel that it's not far away. As I sit with the others, waiting for this Passover meal, I know the time is near. He knows it too. I have seen how he looks at me not with judgment, but with sadness. In a rare moment, I want to go to him and say, "If only you knew what I have done!" And I can imagine him saying, "I do, Judas, I do." And somehow, he would make everything okay.

Then the other voice intrudes. "You are nothing and you are no one. Walk away. A purse full of silver is waiting for you."

21

IN THE GARDEN

- ANDREW -

Luke 22:47-53 | Matthew 26:47-56

MY LUNGS ARE BURNING as I gasp for air. What just happened? I slump against a tree trunk, fighting to calm my heart so I can do something with the memories in my mind. Passover. It's Passover, I have to remind myself. I can still hear the shouts of the Roman soldiers, feel the fear as I watched them grab Jesus. There was chaos, blood, and shouting and Judas was there, but he didn't go to the garden with us. Peter had a sword. Jesus was bleeding after he prayed. He wanted us to pray for him. We couldn't stay awake. So many people showed up...they had weapons. Soldiers and officers. Wait, did they come with Judas?

I'm finally catching my breath. My heartbeat is still fast, but at least I can't feel it hammering in my chest. I look up from where I am hunched over and scan the trees. I see no one and I think I am alone. A thought slams into my head...they took Jesus. They took him. The soldiers took him away. Some of them came for us, too. That's when we ran. As fast as our feet could carry us, we ran. Only...Judas stayed. What is going on?

I force myself to take a deep, ragged breath and piece the night together. I think back to before we gathered for dinner and let the memories come. The quiet of the upstairs room. The surprise of Jesus washing our feet. The taste of the bread and the wine. The sweetness of a hymn sung together. The familiar walk across the Kidron Valley. The unremarkable entrance into Gethsemane. The invitation to pray. The inability to keep my eyes open. The anguish on Jesus' face. His frustration with us. That is where the night shifted. I remember seeing blood on his face when he returned from praying, but where was its source?

Then his words came back to me...

"The time has come for the Son of Man to enter his glory..."

"Don't let your hearts be troubled. Trust in God, and trust also in me. There is more than enough room in my Father's home."

"Soon the world will no longer see me, but you will see me. Since I live, you also will live."

"I have told you these things before they happen so that when they do happen, you will believe. I don't have much more time to talk to you, because the ruler of this world approaches."

"I tell you the truth, you will weep and mourn over what is going to happen to me, but the world will rejoice. You will grieve, but your grief will suddenly turn to wonderful joy."

"Father, the hour has come. Glorify your Son so he can give glory back to you...Now, Father, bring me into the glory we shared before the world began."

The night is still and heavy around me. I push away from the tree and force my feet to move again. Peter. I have to find Peter. They have taken Jesus and are going to put him to death. And I have failed in my quest to walk with him, stay by him, protect him. "Peter will know what to do," I promise myself as I run toward the city.

22

Courageous Coward

- PETER -

Matthew 26:57-75

My skin prickles with awareness. My senses are on high alert. In the distance, I can see Jesus before the religious leaders. Their angry gestures and the faint sounds of their shouted accusations drift across the courtyard to where I stand. John has just joined me and is urging me to move closer. He says he can get us into the courtyard, that he knows someone. I shake him off, and none too gently.

This whole thing is ridiculous! Do they know who they have in there? Do they even have half a clue? They think they have so much power. They think they are so righteous. Do they even understand that with just a word...one word...he could destroy them all? My fists clench at my sides. That's what I would do. Destroy them all. Beginning with that dishonest, conniving high priest. Caiaphas. He's the one who should be on trial. I spit into the dirt.

I notice John coming back my way and slowing as he approaches. He seems concerned. Then I realize the look on my face would probably make a murderer think twice. Anger has risen to take hold of me, and I am fighting to keep it down. The last thing I need is to lose control and cause a scene...I know it is entirely possible.

John tells me we can go in. Anger moves over to welcome fear. The courtyard will be a dangerous place for followers of Jesus. But my need to get close, possibly to hear what is going on, compels me to follow John. We walk up to the door. John talks to the serving girl who is standing there, and she moves to let us in. I focused my eyes on Jesus and trying to hear what is said. Why does he just stand there?

As I pass the girl, she says something quietly. In two more steps, her words register, "This man was one of Jesus' followers!" she exclaimed, tipping her head toward Jesus. I brush her off with a distracted, "Woman, I don't even know him!" and I keep walking. John is a few strides ahead, and I push to catch up. I want to be sure he stays within the group of bystanders so we don't stand out.

The coolness of the night is finally getting to me. I notice the fire the servants and some officers have made, so I step closer to capture its warmth. I am watching closely as people who I assume are false witnesses, paid off by Caiaphas, are brought to share their stories of Jesus. I still haven't heard what the charges against him are. Straining to hear, I notice many around the fire staring at me. The hair on my neck stands up.

"You must be one of them!" one of them says. They all look at me, a couple of them reaching for their weapons. With an ear toward Jesus and an eye on their swords, I hear these words come from my mouth, "No man, I'm not!" They relax, but their hands stay on their swords.

I slowly move away, toward where John is standing. No one says anything else. The night wears on. The religious leaders are yelling at Jesus. They have hit him and spit on him. Only John's hand on my arm keeps me where I am standing. My temples are throbbing with the effort to stay where I am and tears sting behind my eyes. Why doesn't he do something? Why doesn't he speak? What is the charge?

Then I know. I see Caiaphas tear his robe open as he shouts, "He has uttered blasphemy! Why do we need other witnesses?" Someone bumps into me and says, "This must be one of them, because he is a Galilean, too." My temper breaks open on him as I roar, "Man, I don't know what you are talking about."

Then the whole world slows. It's as if all time stands still and with clarity, I hear the religious leaders condemn Jesus to death. In the distance, a rooster crows...my memory jars and I hear Jesus' voice as if he were still standing next to me, "Before the rooster crows, you will deny three times that you even know me." In complete shock and horror, I turn to look across the courtyard at Jesus, tears filling my eyes. I find he's looking at me. The tears spill over as I cave to the emotion of what is before me. I turn and leave as quickly as my feet will move.

23

A Whisper of More
Part 2

- SERVANT GIRL -

Matthew 26:36-75

My brother, sitting on a stump outside the house, got to his feet when he saw me walk out. "Where are you going?" he asked. "Don't you have to clean up the room?"

"Something important is happening," I explained, motioning for him to come with me. He looked unsure, but I was insistent. So, he stepped in alongside me and we quietly followed the men ahead of us. Not wanting to be seen, we slowed so the night could close in around us. We followed in silence as the men left the city and entered the gates of a nearby garden. Stepping off the path and into the trees, we found a spot where we could still see the men, certain they could not see us. A chill in the air seeped through our clothes. Finally, my brother couldn't hold back his curiosity anymore. "Why are we here? It's cold. We have responsibilities elsewhere. We are spying on some random group of travelers." His irritation was evident.

"Their leader is Jesus," I shared. He did not look impressed. "He's the one Papa has been talking about. The teacher, the one that makes the religious leaders nervous. You know. You've heard the stories."

"Yeah, but it still doesn't explain why we are hiding in the bushes."

I was quiet. How could I explain? I heard myself say, "Well, he looked at me and I just knew I had to follow him." It sounded stupid. What serving girl would be so bold? This one, I guess. I was trying to think of what to say to him when his hand shot out and gripped my arm. He looked alarmed. As I followed his gaze, I saw what he was seeing...torches and Roman soldiers entered the grove where the men had been praying and sleeping. The men jumped to their feet, all consumed with nervous energy again. In the middle of them, Jesus stood calm and composed.

We watched as an unarmed man (hadn't I seen him in the upper room?) walked out from behind the soldiers, approached Jesus, and greeted him with a kiss. Then chaos ensued. The soldiers moved forward, hands on their swords and chains in their hands, just as one of Jesus' followers lunged forward with his sword, taking a swing at the men. He injured one of them, who gripped the side of his head as blood ran through his fingers. Moving through the confusion, Jesus touched the bleeding man's head at the same time that he told his follower to put the sword away. The injured man removed his hands from his head and the blood was gone. The wound was completely gone. The astonished look on his face helped us to know what we had just seen was true. Jesus had healed him.

Then the moment passed, and the soldiers were taking Jesus into custody, placing the chains on his hands and leading him away. His followers turned and ran away from the soldiers, confused and afraid of what was happening. We stayed rooted where we were, hoping to escape detection. As the grove emptied, we turned to follow the soldiers. We were so involved now going home didn't seem like an option.

We noticed some leaders from the synagogue among the group of soldiers that were leading Jesus away. Where were they taking him? Why had he been arrested? We made it as far as the outer area of the temple courts, just as they led Jesus inside. Others had gathered in the area and we noticed a fire off to the side. We headed over to it just to warm ourselves. My brother and I had yet to speak. I'm sure he was trying to make sense of all we had seen, just like I was.

Enjoying the warmth of the fire, I noticed a man walk up to warm his hands. I snuck a look at him and was struck by how familiar he seemed. It took a while for me to put it all together, but the more that time passed, the more confident I became he was one of the followers of Jesus. I was sure I had seen him in the upper room at the Passover meal. Was he the one who refused to let Jesus wash his feet? I couldn't be sure. But he definitely was the one who injured the man in the grove. I nudged my brother and whispered, "I think he's one of them." My brother frowned at me. We sat there quietly. I looked at the man whenever I was sure he was looking the other way. Each time I saw his face, I was certain he was one of them. Finally, I blurted out, "You were one of those with Jesus the Galilean."

His head snapped in my direction and he growled as he grabbed my arm. "I don't know what you're talking about," and with that, he left the fire and moved closer to the gate. Curious onlookers followed him, but I stayed where I was because my brother was holding my arm. "Why did you say that?" he hissed.

"I don't know. I didn't think about it. I just said it. I had to say it," I shrugged helplessly.

He pulled me away from the fire. "Let's get back to the room, clean it up and go home before someone notices we are gone or, worse, someone here comes looking for us after you provoked that man!" He was right; we needed to get somewhere safe. I really don't know what possessed me to speak. With unexplained emotion swirling inside me, my brother's grip on my arm, and the sound of a rooster crowing not too far away, we turned in the direction of the upper room and walked as quickly as our feet would carry us.

24

WASHING OF HANDS

- PONTIUS PILATE -

Matthew 27:11-26 | Luke 23:1-12 | John 19:1-16

SOMEHOW, TIME HAS BEEN suspended. Shouting and chaos erupt, but retreating into my mind has sheltered me. The lives of two men hang in the balance. I have the power to sentence either to death. Usually this does not phase me, but today is different. I wish her messenger had never come. Or that he had arrived sooner, like hours ago. But that was not the case and now her warning stares up at me from the parchment I hold. "Leave that innocent man alone." Her words echo relentlessly in my head. Oh, Claudia. I have so many questions for you that will never be asked.

The problem is that I agree with her assessment. This Jesus has undoubtedly done something, just not what the Jewish leaders accuse him of doing. In my opinion, he is no traitor. Standing a distance off from me, he is as peaceful now as he was when I questioned him. Honestly, I would not have bothered. But those zealous Sadducees would not relent. My ultimate job here in Jerusalem is to keep the peace. If I want to keep my job, wealth, and life, then I will keep the peace. At all costs. It was my sole aim when I agreed to interrogate him.

He stood there, calm, quiet. The priests were hurling accusations at him, trying to convince me and provoke him. Finally, having had enough, I raised my hand for silence. The angry voices faded out. We stood in silence as I considered what I would say to this man to whom I had absolutely no allegiance. Oh, I knew who he was. A teacher. Some said a healer. But he was not a troublemaker, and I had not concerned myself with him. Until the religious fanatics demanded my attention.

Annoyed, I began with this question, "Are you king of the Jews?" using the term the Sadducees invented to bring him to trial. I heard a sharp intake of breath from Caiaphas when I said that title out loud. Good. He had certainly disrupted my life. I did not mind in the least disrupting his. I stared intently at Jesus, waiting for his answer, trying to discern the substance of the man.

"You have said it," he replied quietly. My annoyance rose. What kind of answer is that? Does he know who I am? Does he know the danger he is in? I took a breath and tried again.

"Don't you hear all these charges they are bringing against you?" He said nothing. Unbelievable. What kind of person refuses to defend himself in the face of possible death? So it was for the next few minutes. I asked questions, and he gave non-committal answers if he answered at all. "Why don't you talk to me? Don't you realize that I have the power to release you or crucify you?" His only response? "You would have no power over me unless it were given to you from above."

Interestingly, I found the more time I spent with him, the less annoyed I became. Instead, I was intrigued. I realized I was wishing for more time with him...just him. But I did not have that luxury. I looked at Caiaphas and said, "I find nothing wrong with this man!" The religious leaders would not accept my answer. With vehemence, they insisted, "But he is causing riots by his teaching wherever he goes—all over Judea, from Galilee to Jerusalem!"

Two things in this statement caught my attention: riots and Galilee. Riots in my jurisdiction I cannot have. But neither do I want to find Jesus guilty of such a minor charge. I seize on Galilee because that is outside my territory. Galilee is under Herod Antipas' control. Herod, who happens to be in Jerusalem. I see my escape and say to the leaders, "Oh, is he a Galilean?" I turn to my servant and have him arrange the transfer of Jesus to Herod's court for a verdict.

I thought that would be the end, but it was not. Jesus was no more talkative with Herod, who, like me, found nothing punishable in the man. What seemed like only hours after I thought I had relieved myself of Jesus, he reappeared at the Praetorium. Before meeting with Jesus a second time, I called the Sadducees together to give them my verdict. They were not happy. "You brought this man to me, accusing him of leading a revolt. I have examined him thoroughly on this point in your presence and find him innocent. Herod came to the same conclusion and sent him back to us. Nothing this man has done calls for the death penalty. So I will have him flogged, and then I will release him."

Then all hell broke loose. And I am currently standing in the midst of it, desperately playing the events through my mind, testing all strategies and struggling to ignore the warning message from my wife that so eloquently matches my observations and fear. "Leave that innocent man alone." I am trying to. I really am. But the crowd is pulsing with pent up energy. If I don't dispel it before it spills over into certain destruction, I will be the one to answer for it. Keep the peace. Free the innocent man. Keep the peace. Leave the innocent man alone. In a moment that some would define as a strength and others as weakness, I decide to keep the peace.

But then I see it. The way out. Barabbas and a Passover custom. I could let them choose who to release in keeping with the custom. Then it would not be my decision at all; I could honor both my wife and my conscience. "Which one do you want me to release to you - Barabbas or Jesus who is called the Messiah?" I asked. The crowd rebelled, and the shouts came one after another for me to release Barabbas, another criminal in my jail. I could not understand it. Barabbas was actually dangerous. Violent. But

Jesus? I do not think I have met a more peace-filled man. To my surprise, they chose Barabbas.

"Then what should I do with Jesus, who is called Messiah?"

Nothing prepared me for their response. "Crucify him!" It defied logic.

"Why? What crime has he committed?"

But the unruly mob shouted all the more, "Crucify him! Crucify him!"

This was wrong. I knew it in my bones. But the phrase "keep the peace" kept floating through my head. I turned away from the crowd and asked a servant to bring a bowl of water to me. Something in me needed to distance myself from this verdict. I kept reminding myself it was their choice, not mine. When the water bowl arrived, I made a show of washing my hands in it as I stated as loudly and clearly as I could, "I am innocent of this man's blood. The responsibility is yours!"

I left the portico as quickly as I could, pausing briefly to give the order to remand the custody of Jesus to the religious leaders along with twelve Roman soldiers as guards. As I walked past Jesus, I paused again, looking into the face of this man who, unexpectedly, I admired. I said nothing. Neither did he. He did not have to. With just a look and no words at all, he set me free.

25

A Boy and His Lunch

John 6:1-15 | Matthew 14:13-21

Being young is hard. There is so much that I want to do and see, but I have to wait for permission first. Permission from grown-ups. Permission from my dad. I am waiting for that permission now. He is thinking.

I suppose he is thinking that a boy like me has no place on a hill like Calvary. But today is not most days. Today, they took Jesus of Nazareth to Calvary to die. I still do not understand why.

The past week has been a blur. Many people are talking about him. About Jesus. My ears have been open…listening to talk, to arguments, to rumors. I have heard him called many names…everything from king to blasphemer. This is where being young has been an advantage. No one has noticed the young boy on the edge of a crowd, of a gathering, of a room filled with adults trying to discern what to believe about Jesus. In this way, I have enjoyed being overlooked. But I wish I had a voice in their wondering, grappling, and fear about Jesus and the claims surrounding him. I could tell them who he is. I know.

My mind goes back to another hill. My father and I had walked a long way to hear Jesus teach. It was dry and dusty. Hot. Thousands had gathered with curious minds, wanting to decide whether Jesus was the promised Messiah, or just an outstanding teacher. There were so many people gathered on the hillside, primarily men. But some of them had brought their families, too.

Children and women were present in a way they could not have been if Jesus had been teaching in the temple. I noticed many people who were not Jewish. It occurs to me now that perhaps Jesus meant that to happen. Maybe he taught outside on purpose so that everyone could hear. So unlike the Jewish leaders of our synagogue.

I could hear his voice, clear and strong, though we were far from him. I noticed some men gathered around him, trying to keep the crowds from pressing in too close, holding back mothers who were bold to draw near with their children. I asked my father about this group of men who seemed to be in service to Jesus. He told me they were his followers, his disciples.

As I listened to Jesus teach, I found I wanted to be his follower. His teaching was simple, a message a boy like me could understand. I listened, mesmerized by this teacher, until the grumbling of my stomach interrupted my thoughts. I looked at the sun in the sky and realized it was well past the mid-day meal. I reached for the food my mother had given me when we left home that morning. A simple lunch of bread and fish.

As I opened the sack, one follower of Jesus came through the crowd looking for food. I stood up and offered my lunch. He walked over to me, looked in the bag, shrugged his shoulders, and accepted my offer. "It's not much," I said quietly. He smiled and said, "It's more than nothing." I watched him walk away, wondering what he would do with my food. Then it occurred to me he might bring it to Jesus. The thought pulled me from my place beside my father and, without realizing it, I ran after the man who had claimed my lunch for Jesus.

But it wasn't a lunch for Jesus. My bread and fish became so much more. In the hands of Jesus, it became lunch for EVERYONE. I watched my lunch multiplied repeatedly until everyone on the hillside had fish and bread. Thousands of us had fish and bread, and some were still left over. He fed us physically that day. He fed me spiritually. I know who Jesus is. He revealed himself to me on that hillside.

So I wait for permission to join him on another hillside. Some might say a boy has no place there today. But Jesus doesn't see me as a boy. He sees me as a follower. One who has seen, recognized and chosen to believe. If anyone asks me, I will tell them who Jesus is. He is the one who gathers all people—young, old, male, female, Jewish, non-Jewish—all people to himself. He is the Messiah.

26

CENTURION'S CONSCIENCE

Mark 15:37-39 | Luke 23:44-49

I DIDN'T WANT THIS tour of duty. I was happier with my battalion back home. Close to my wife...my kids. Near to my friends. But when Rome calls, obedience is the only choice. I arrived in Jerusalem just last week. Crowds were already streaming into the city. Cheaters and thieves among them, plotting to overcharge, steal, bribe and kill anyone who got in their way. There was perfect cover for them in these large crowds. I was bitter. I was angry. Who wants to be in Jerusalem during the Passover celebration of those Jews and their zealots? Not me. No, not me.

Barely received by the other soldiers on duty, I could feel their cold stares and recognition of me as a temporary recruit from some outlying location. They did not hide their contempt. I pretended I didn't care. I soon found I did not like their way of soldiering. Keep the peace? That, I can do. Arrest those in violation of Roman law? I can do that, too. Abuse my power to take advantage of others? That is a place I cannot go.

Yet I am standing on this lonely, forsaken hill they call Calvary. We await death's arrival to claim the three condemned souls on those crosses. What a way to die. There must be a less gruesome way to punish. I hate this job. Today, I don't even really like myself. I stood by and watched and kept the crowd at bay, as these men were beaten, degraded, brutalized and nailed to wooden beams. Nails? Until today, I thought they used rope. I guess I am a simple country soldier. I've seen plenty of death, but this? This is different from taking the life of your enemy in combat. I may not have driven those spikes, but I certainly am part of this crucifixion. It makes my stomach turn. I try to think of my wife, but then I make myself stop. I don't want to bring her to this hill with me.

From where I stand, I can see these men as they struggle to breathe on their crosses. I can see the other soldiers gambling at their feet. I survey the crowd and see curiosity on some faces, satisfaction in others, and extreme anguish in a few. There is a woman crumpled to the ground who seems unable to look up. Her grief emanates from her body. Close by, there is another woman in black. Silent tears are on her face as she makes herself look at the one in the middle. A man stands beside her with his arm around her, the moment's pain clearly etched on his face. This must be family. Only family could stand and witness what they must witness.

My gaze shifts to the religious leaders gathered off to the side. A small group of men who clearly feel superior. I shake my head. These Jewish people are so fanatical about their faith. It doesn't appeal to me. Rules, rules, and more rules. My world as a soldier has plenty of that. No, if I were part of a religious movement, compassion would draw me, not more rules.

The Jewish leaders seem satisfied with what is taking place and look like they are planning to leave the hill. I know they are concerned about the one in the middle...the one I have heard others call Jesus. I saw the sign they put above him in mockery...King of the Jews. I allow myself to think about that. What does it mean? Clearly, he is not really a king. As a soldier of Rome, I would know if we had captured a king and were putting him to death. The crowd gathered here would be ten times bigger and much more unruly. This is no king. I look at him and find he is looking at me. I stop breathing for a moment. Such compassion in that look! I feel as if he really sees me. Then he looks away.

What just happened? My heart is racing as my mind grapples with those fleeting seconds in time. Who is he? How can he look at me, a stranger, for mere moments and leave me feeling as if I have known him my whole life? I suddenly feel exposed standing on that hill. For all my gear as a soldier, I feel as if I am laid bare. It shakes me to the core and forces me to look at the man they have called king. He talks to one thief hanging next to him with great effort. What is he saying? Are they words of compassion that match the gift he has just given me? Who is this man?

I want to draw closer. I find I want to hear him speak. I want to talk to those gathered at the foot of his cross, but I dare not move. I have a job to do. They have assigned me a post. Out of obedience, I stay where I am. But I long to be obedient to another and cannot even say whence this desire comes. I have never questioned my call before. I am a soldier. *I am a soldier*. But today, the one with eyes of compassion has seen me as a man. He has seen me. Somehow, in the middle of dying, he has seen all of me.

I notice the sky is darkening in an eerie way. I look around, but there is no explanation. Only fear and anxiety. The religious leaders are hurrying away. I step toward the crosses. I know I am not supposed to leave my post, but I am drawn anyway. The darkness is deepening, and the cries of the women intensify. But I stare at the man in the middle...the one who has seen me.

Unbelievably, he raises his head and says to the sky, "Father, I entrust my spirit into your hands." With that, his head falls forward, and I know he is gone. The sadness overwhelms me and I wish I could have gone with him. I say out loud what I am thinking, "This man truly was the Son of God!"

I stare at him on the cross and think about this man of compassion, the one who has seen me. I could have followed this man.

27

REDEEMED

- MARY MAGDALENE -

John 19:25-30

THE SMELL OF THE earth fills me as I kneel on the hillside. I had long ago stopped looking at him on the cross. The weight, my grief, my sorrow, the exhaustion living in my bones made it impossible to stand any longer. I sank to my knees and fell forward, face to the ground, hands grabbing fists full of dirt. I have been like this for a long time now. I wish with every fiber of my being that I was not on this hill, that none of us were. That he was not up on that cross. That we were back in the countryside somewhere safe. Somewhere filled with sunshine and warmth and the smell of the sea on the wind. The coldness of the dirt, the stiffness in my knees and my back tell me the truth. With every ragged breath, I can smell earth.

My tears will not stop falling. I glance at his mother, so faithful in her prayers. She never takes her eyes from him. I am not that strong. I have never been that strong, except for a brief moment when he restored my hope, when he gave me value, when his eyes and words showed me I could be loved. My mind goes back to when I was ravaged by demons, unable to live life among others. Feared by everyone, even the religious leaders. But not Jesus. He was different. He stepped toward me. He commanded, and the demons listened. He set me free in so many ways.

I had hope then, but only agony now. He is dying, leaving. It hurts more than I would have imagined. It crushes the heart within my chest.

All I can do is stare at the mud my tears create as they mingle with the earth. I try to raise my face to his. Just one last time to see him, to know him. But I am weak. I cannot bear to look at him on that cross. To see what they have done to him. The blood. The bruising. Roman brutality on full display. Sanctioned by the religious leaders. The beating would have been enough, but this? THIS?? Crucified with criminals? The soldiers are actually gambling for what is left of his clothes. How can it be happening this way? Why didn't someone intervene? How will we possibly live life without him in it? The devastation I am experiencing is crippling. It keeps me tethered to the earth.

Time slows, creeping at an excruciating pace. I wish it would stop altogether. Better yet, I want to turn it back. But I know that is not possible. I lift my head enough to glance around the hill, but not at the cross, not at him hanging there on the cross, dying. I shiver. It is getting darker, colder. I hear voices on the hill beginning to rise. People are commenting with fear on the increasing darkness. They hurry to leave, religious leaders included, concern draped across their shoulders. They do not want to be here. I don't blame them, and yet I do.

In the rising commotion, I hear his voice from the cross, quiet and determined.

"It is finished."

The thought echoes through my head with lightning speed...

Finished

Complete

Done

Silenced

Over

Accomplished.

His words rattle my soul. I force myself to look up at him, and just as I do, his eyes meet mine. Without a word, I know there is more. His eyes remind me: I have value, I am loved. His words linger in my mind. As his eyes close and his head slumps forward, I know it has just begun.

28

IN THE GAP

- MARY, THE MOTHER OF JESUS -

John 19:25-27 | Luke 23:44-49

I WAS JUST A child when I said yes. Eager to please. Easily connected to my faith in God. As a young girl, very little stood in the way of my seeing you, sensing your presence in my life, hearing your voice. You called me to an important task...one I would never have imagined would be mine. Looking back, I can't believe the time has gone by so quickly. You threw me into controversy and I knew I could endure with you at my side. I pray I have done well the task you asked of me.

But it is not over yet. This is the hardest of all the trials this heart has had to survive. I know he has asked you to let the cup pass from him. But that has not been your will. So I do not ask for this cup to pass from me, either. Even so, he is my son, too. You have watched him from afar for thirty-three years. I have held him close. I know how his skin feels. I know what his laughter sounds like. I remember the smell of fresh air, sweat, and little boy. I can almost recall it if I close my eyes.

But I will not close them. I will stand to watch as long as he breathes, though it is tearing me apart. At lightning speed, the memories come fast and furious: a newborn in a stall prepared for animals, an unexpected visit from far away kings, a frantic flight to Egypt, a young boy lost on our trip to Jerusalem...this mother holding him close through all of that. My arms ache to hold him.

Never have I questioned you and I struggle not to do so now. I am beyond thankful that your messenger did not reveal this plan when he arrived at my home all those years ago. His visit was disturbing and reassuring all at the same time. I remember feeling peaceful and wondering why I wasn't terrified. I feel that same peace now even though my heart is breaking to watch him. I know I am not alone. My agony pales compared to yours.

His words from the cross have been so gut-wrenching to hear. He wonders why you have forsaken him. He entrusts me to the care of one of his closest earthly friends. He has blessed and welcomed a thief into his kingdom. His love is outrageous. His strength and singular focus was so totally overwhelming. I see in him characteristics that must be yours alone. I have always seen that.

More memories press in...coming to the aid of the host of a wedding, patiently training and leading his group of twelve, restoring health and wholeness, walking on water, welcoming children, restoring the dignity of a woman who had none...she kneels in the dirt beside me now. And then there is Lazarus. Who cannot but follow him after such a display of kingdom authority?

Kingdom authority. That is what's happening now, isn't it? Your kingdom—your authority—meeting my broken and needy earth. The cries from a week ago echo through my mind. Hosanna, save us.

You have darkened the sky, and the ground has trembled. I know you are here, though I cannot see you. I wish I could see you though I know it would destroy me to do so. I know your messengers are here, too, though I cannot see them either. Though my eyes cannot perceive the heavenly realm, I know it is here. I can see it on the face of my son. He knows you are near.

God in heaven, I have done what you asked of me. With all that I am, I have loved him with a mother's love...all the while knowing he was never really mine. In this moment, I am glad he is yours because you can redeem him from the agony of this crucifixion. I know he understands you must look the other way from his words. But that is a place in which I can stand. I can continue to look, watch, and love while you suspend your love for the briefest moments. I will watch for both of us until he passes from this world and from my embrace into yours. Father, into your hands I commend his spirit.

29

MOVED BY MERCY

- JOSEPH OF ARIMATHEA -

Luke 23:50-54

MY LIFE IS AT risk. All that I have worked for, and trained for, since a child is in the balance. Yet I cannot hide in the shadows any longer. I have been witness to the most heinous crime. No, not witness...participant. As a young Jewish scholar, never would I have imagined the word of the Lord to be so misused, so totally ignored. As I stand on this hill and watch the man I believe is the Son of God struggle for his last breaths, I find my feet carefully stepping away from my colleagues. What was once a prestigious title for me, the culmination of all that my father wanted for me, tastes sour. I wish I could spit it out.

My eyes stay focused on the cross, though I know that the rest of the leaders from the synagogue are preparing to leave. Their smugness rankles. I hear their pride, and remember the insults they spat at him just hours earlier. My voice did not join theirs, but I am guilty by association. I want to rip this robe from my body. I am miserable. The man who was to be the savior of the world is close, oh so close, to death. He can save no one now. And I don't feel worthy of being saved.

There was a time, not too long ago, when I felt free. I felt on top of the world. I was respected. Important. People listened to my wise words and acted on them. I interpreted scripture for use in disputes. I interpreted the law. I enjoyed the benefits of my upbringing and studies. My knowledge of God's word was complete, nearly every word committed to memory. I was someone to be emulated. I looked good to the public eye. But I know now that it was a farce. I was nothing more than an empty shell, going through the motions I had been taught but not engaging my faith.

Then my path crossed with Jesus. That encounter wrecked me for the job that I loved. Suddenly, the law I had worked so hard to uphold didn't seem as important as mercy. Jesus taught me the power of love, forgiveness, and walking in his footsteps. Still, I couldn't walk away from my life. I still haven't walked away. I am so at war with myself as I stare at the cross. The rest of the members of the Sanhedrin are leaving. The increasing darkness in the middle of the day unnerves them. I can feel that it means something, too. I should go, but my feet stay.

I see Jesus raise his head and speak to his mother. Selfishly, I wish he would speak to me. I need him to speak to me. I have failed in the worst way. I wish I were on that cross. I won't look away. It is so hard to watch, but it is the only way to punish myself. I didn't speak for him when I could have. I didn't stop the injustice that nailed him where he is. I am a coward. My feet keep me rooted where I am.

Then he looks at me, and I am astonished to receive what he has to give. He does not see me as he should. He does not see me the way I do. Instead, he offers compassion. Mercy. Grace. Forgiveness. One by one, they roll over me, washing me from head to toe. His love makes me better than I really am. My knees buckle under the comprehension that Jesus sees me as I want to be seen...his follower.

I stumble forward and catch myself in time to see him look to the sky and say, "It is finished." The truth of those words presses into me. It really is finished. I thought I knew what freedom was, but I now experience so much more. It is finished. My betrayal of him is over. My guilt lifted.

My shame silenced. My emptiness filled. My identity recreated. I am his follower. I do not need to live the lie that has been my life.

Tears are streaming down my face. I realize Jesus has died, and I have been given life in his death. I know now what I will do to thank him. I will go to Pilate. I will ask for the privilege of removing Jesus' body from the cross and preparing it for burial. New life is coursing through my veins. I look across the crowd gathered and find there is one other who stands as I do in awe of this collision of heaven and earth. Nicodemus. He looks at me and nods. I know I am not alone. He will join me as we honor the body of the one we took too long to serve.

But I serve him now. I am Joseph of Arimathea. I am a follower of Jesus.

30

SUPPOSED TO WIN

- NICODEMUS -

John 19:38-39 | Matthew 27:50-56

THIS ISN'T RIGHT. IT'S not how it was supposed to happen. How did they lose control so quickly? How is it that my colleagues have been so hard of heart? I have talked to Jesus myself. Shared my concerns. Asked my questions. Gave voice to my wondering. He listened well. He heard every word. He taught me to believe. For a while now, I have known him not just as a Jewish rabbi...I know him as the Messiah. But nothing I have said in the assembly or inside conversations has reached their hearts. Only one believes as I do—Joseph who comes from Arimathea. Pride blinds everyone else.

And so I stand on this wind-blown hill watching him die. Golgotha...The Skull. Indeed. It is a place of death and misery so dark that the sun cannot even shine today. I am cold all the way to my core, but it's not the weather that makes me so. I long for the warmth of the conversations I had with him. While I came to him as a possible enemy, he always welcomed me as a friend. I vented my frustrations, and he lent me his peace. I begged for answers and he provided a way out of my sin. I glance at his battered body on the cross and am grateful for the gift he has given me.

I don't want him to die. I don't want to lose him. I need the hope he brings and the strength he gives.

I'm an old man. And at this moment, life is way too hard. I wonder if I have the energy for it. I have hidden my true self from my colleagues. I have hidden my true self from his followers. I'm tired of hiding. Tired of pretending. Tired of fearing what it would mean to let the world know I have put my faith in the most remarkable man I have ever known. The one who suffers, the one who bleeds, the one who gasps for air on the cross before me. Don't go, Jesus. Don't die. Win. I want you to win. You have to win. You have to WIN.

Suddenly, there is chaos. The ground is shaking, people are yelling. The soldiers jump up from their gambling and grab their weapons. The sky is getting even darker and a runner from the temple arrives out of breath with the news that the curtain barring entrance to the Holy of Holies has torn in two pieces from top to bottom. Another messenger arrives to say that graves in the cemetery have opened and people have come back to life. A soldier drops his spear and mutters, "This man truly was the Son of God!" Fear grips the religious leaders as they hastily turn to leave. A voice in my head cries, "What have we done?"

I look to where his followers gathered. They refuse to leave. Even as everything comes undone around them, they are resolute. The mother of Jesus stands with a strength that can't even be human. The one they call Mary Magdalene is on her knees, consumed with her anguish. I look for Joseph, but he is gone. I assume he left with the religious leaders. I decide that I will head toward the temple and look for him. I glance back to the cross as the rumbling of the earth lessens and see Jesus' lifeless body. My breath catches in my throat and tears come as I whisper, "You were supposed to win."

31

LINEN AND SPICES

- MARY MAGDALENE -

John 19:38-42 | Matthew 27: 57-61

PEOPLE HAVE BEEN MOVING around me for quite some time now. I literally cannot stand. The ground is no longer shaking, but I am. I watched him die...and here I live. It's not fair. It's not right. His life was worth so much more than mine. He can do more for the world than this broken mess of a human being can do. I'm weary to the core. Every part of me aches. I have cried every single tear I have. The skin on my face feels tight with all the dried tears and dirt covering it. I feel like I should attempt to move, but I do not want to.

"Mary," I feel a hand on my shoulder as I hear the strong voice of the woman whose name I share. "Come with me. They are taking him off the cross. Come with me. I have to be near him, see him one more time." She's pulling at my sleeve, begging me to rise. I'll do it for her...and for him.

Pain shoots through me as I uncoil my legs tucked beneath my body for hours. My feet tingle and prickle as if I am walking on glass. She lends me her arm, but I find it's not enough to pull me out of the dirt where I crouch. Then, a stronger arm reaches down. I am grateful as John's arm around my waist lifts me to my feet and stays there to help me walk. We are silent, we three, as we move slowly toward the cross while it seems everyone else is moving away.

They have removed the spikes from his hands and feet, leaving behind holes where no holes should ever be. His skin is bruised underneath the blood that is drying. His eyes are closed. The hideous crown of thorns was removed and cast off to the side. I stumble as I notice the wound in his side made by a soldier's spear. Why? Oh, Jesus, why?

His mother kneels beside him, a hand resting on his chest as she bows her head to pray. I do not listen because I know a mother's prayer for her son is hers alone. Words to be shared with God only. But I can sense their weight as she silently cries, tears splashing off her face as she gently rocks back and forth. I stand closer to John, grateful for his presence and friendship. We wait with patience and understanding as a mother says goodbye.

Time is passing, but we are not aware of it. The moment is too intense, personal, and painful for something like time to make a mark. So it startles us when a man appears with a cloth to wrap up the body of Jesus. And another man is with him with spices and oils for burial. A soft cry escapes my lips as I realize they mean to honor Jesus and his mother with a proper Jewish burial. I look more closely at these two men and find that I know one of them. Nicodemus. I remember Jesus talking about him. The other man is helping Mary to her feet and bringing her over to us. He tells us he is Joseph and Pilate has given him permission to prepare Jesus' body for burial.

We stand in awe of this gift and watch as these two men carefully, gently, and adequately go about their work. It is an act of love. It's an act of devotion. There is an urgency and passion about what they are doing and I sense this means more to them than they will ever say. They lift Jesus between them and we walk along toward a garden. We come to a brand new tomb and sit on a stone opposite the grave as the men carry Jesus in. Moments later, they come out and roll a massive stone together in front of the tomb. Everyone turns to go, but I stay where I am. I cannot go just yet. Mary understands and squeezes my arm to let me know. And soon I am alone. I draw my knees to my chin and sit with my arms around them. I feel hollow. I am exhausted. My stomach protests from lack of food. Darkness is falling and the Sabbath has arrived. But I cannot go just yet because I do not know how to say goodbye.

32

A Whisper of More
Part 3

- SERVANT GIRL -

Matthew 27:32-56

THE MORNING DAWNED QUIET and normal. We all went about our morning routines with efficiency. My brother and I had been chastised for taking so long to get home the night before. My mother assumed I had been lazy at my tasks, and that's why we came home late. We didn't correct her. We didn't talk about what really happened. We had agreed not to tell anyone. And so, the morning progressed as it normally would have.

It was late in the morning when my father returned home. He was earlier than usual for the noon meal and he arrived with a sense of urgency. "They've arrested him," he told my mother. My brother and I froze.

"Arrested who?" my mother asked.

"Jesus of Nazareth. The teacher I have been telling you about. The one the religious leaders dislike so much."

"What has he done to get arrested?" my mother inquired.

"That's the problem," he said. "There don't really seem to be any charges. At least, not anything truthful. They have had him on trial all morning, before the Sanhedrin and the Governor. Rumor is that the Pharisees want him killed, but don't want to be responsible for his death. They are trying to get Pilate to sentence him."

My brother and I added this information to what we had experienced the night before.

"Well," my mother began as she wiped her hands on her apron, "I wasn't expecting you this early for lunch, but I can get something together quickly if you just want to sit and relax." She turned toward the table and the bowls and plates covered with a cloth. I picked up the water pitcher and a cup to pour a drink for my father.

"No time to eat a full meal," my dad responded. He walked up next to her and reached for the loaf of bread. As he tore a chunk off the loaf, she asked, "What will you do?"

Halfway to the door, he spoke over his shoulder, "I'm heading to the temple courts to find out what they plan to do with this Jesus." And with that, he was out the door. My brother looked at me and I knew what he was thinking. He walked outside. I waited a few minutes and followed. He was standing a little way up the path and I moved quickly to catch up. "Are you sure?" I asked. He nodded confidently, and we began walking the same road my dad had taken only minutes earlier. It wasn't until we were down the street from our house that I noticed I was still carrying the pitcher and cup from home.

The streets were much more crowded today. We could hear shouting and commotion coming from several directions. The closer we got to the temple, the bigger and louder the crowds grew. We noticed some movement at the street corner ahead of us and hurried to see what was happening. I will never erase the next three hours from my mind.

At a distance, we saw a man struggling to carry a cross. We had arrived in time to see a crucifixion procession. I was about to turn and walk away. It was not something I wanted to see. But at the last moment, I saw that the man under the weight of the cross was Jesus. A small cry escaped my lips as my feet became rooted where they were. I simply stared. He looked awful. Bent over by the weight of the wood on his back, he barely stayed on his feet. One agonizing step after another, he slowly made his way in our direction. Horrified by what I was seeing, I felt my stomach turn. Soldiers were yelling at him to move, and I jumped at the sound of a whip cracking near his head. Someone should help him. Why wasn't anyone helping him?

He stumbled and nearly lost his balance. With what seemed like super-human ability, he stayed on his feet and inched a little closer. He had a crown of thorns on his head, and I could see his back was bleeding from his injuries. Tears stung my eyes. My heart continued to cry, "Help him. Someone, please, help him." But no one did. No one. People lined the streets, but no one moved to help.

He was almost even with where we were standing when the last of his strength gave out and he tumbled to the ground; the cross sliding from his back. His face rested in the dirt and the dust moved with each ragged breath he exhaled. The soldiers were trying to get him to stand, but he just couldn't. One soldier looked in our direction and summoned the man standing next to us. They told the man to carry the cross for Jesus. With no option to disobey a soldier's orders, the man walked over to the imposing piece of wood to shoulder it and carry it for him.

As he wrestled with the wood, I slipped from the crowd and kneeled in the dirt before Jesus. I poured a cup of water from the pitcher I was carrying and offered it to him. He gratefully drank what he could through his dry, cracked lips. Tears stung the corners of my eyes as he looked at me for only a moment before the soldiers pushed us apart and yelled at him to stand. Summoning his small amount of strength, Jesus struggled to his feet and continued to walk.

The crowd moved on. My brother joined me where I was in the dirt. We couldn't believe what we had seen. He put his arm around me as my tears fell. Why was this happening? What had Jesus done wrong? My father had said they did not even have a truthful charge against him. How is it that Jesus had been so wounded and abused by the Romans and ordered to death on a cross? That kind of death was for the worst of the worst, not for people who had done nothing wrong.

I felt my tears continue to fall. My brother held me as I cried. Neither one of us spoke. It was the hardest thing I have ever seen or had to process. I found words failed. There really was nothing I could say at the moment that seemed important to say. We turned and walked. Without realizing it at first, we walked toward the hill where crucifixions take place. When I realized where we were headed, my steps faltered. "I don't think I can," I said quietly to my brother.

We could see the hill from where we were. Off in the distance, we could barely see a crowd gathering and discern the shapes of the crosses as they were raised in the air. I was glad. I knew I could not bear to watch anyone die, especially Jesus. I didn't even know him, but from the look he gave me back in the upper room, something was stirring inside me. Without explanation, I knew he was different. He was something more than anyone I had ever met.

To this nobody servant girl he gave a sense of value that hadn't existed before. For one moment in time, I was more than just me. And he was the reason. It felt like being found. Only, I didn't even know I was lost. That he was dying on a cross in the distance brought such immense grief to me I could barely breathe. To lose him now seemed unfair and cruel. I leaned against my brother, hoping to gain some of his strength.

He gently encouraged me to turn away and head toward home. It was then that I noticed how dark the sky was becoming. Even though it wasn't windy like it gets when a storm moves in, the sun suddenly darkened. My brother and I both looked at the sky. As we did, we felt the earth shake. I had experienced nothing like it before. As disconcerting as it was, I knew it had something to do with Jesus dying. After a while, it got brighter, and the shaking stopped. We walked silently toward home, feeling the weight of the day press heavily into us.

It wouldn't be until later that night that my dad would return home, confirming all we already knew had happened. Jesus had died on the cross. The sky was mysteriously dark. The ground shook and people were filled with fear. In addition to that came the news that the curtain in the temple that separates people from the Holy of Holies...the room where God's word is kept, the room where God himself meets with only the high priest...the curtain tore into two pieces from top to bottom with no one near enough to be responsible. The Holy of Holies was laid open for all to see. My dad couldn't stop talking about it. The fear and wonder in his voice were unmistakable. Something was dramatically different, and we were only beginning to understand what it was.

Section 4: LIFE RETURNS

Remember, you are held safe. You are loved. You are protected. You are in communion with God and with those whom God has sent you. What is of God will last. It belongs to the eternal life. Choose it, and it will be yours.

Henri Nouwen
The Inner Voice of Love

33

Lost or Found

- ANDREW -

I DO NOT KNOW if I can adequately describe the last few days. As I sit in the darkness of this room, listening to the sounds of exhausted men who have finally been rewarded with sleep, my mind still races. There is a strange sense of peace settling around me, like a light morning fog waiting for the rising sun's warmth to disperse it. There it is. Warmth. That's what is missing. Oh, it's not that it's overly cold in this room. My cloak is on the floor next to me. I know I could wrap it around my body if I need it. No. I am not talking about that kind of warmth. I am talking about the warmth of life that produces things like joy, laughter, and hope. It's the warmth that tells us we're going to be okay. It gives the comfort that beckons you to keep going, so you do. Because you know you are safe. And you step out, believing it is the right thing to do. Thinking there is an adventure worth living. Believing you will make a discovery about the world.

That kind of warmth is not something I feel right now. Sitting here, in the depth of the unknown, a coldness seeps in. It brings the opposite of warmth. It ushers in sadness, tears, and despair. We do not know if we are going to be okay. At any moment, the Roman soldiers could come for us the way they came for Jesus. We do not dare to go out. We have been huddled in this room, doors closed, windows shuttered since they took his body down from the cross. How long has it been? Ten hours? Eleven?

Time is so elusive right now. It feels like an eternity. With a deep pang of anguish, I realize that the warmth I am missing is Jesus.

I watch my brother Peter as he sleeps. Even in sleep, he is restless. I call to mind his frenzy when they arrested Jesus in the garden. Big and brash as ever, drawing his sword and taking a swing at the nearest soldier. His explosive passion was immediately backed down by the penetrating calm of Jesus as he healed the man that Peter tried to kill. I picked up the sword Peter dropped and held it at my side as Peter's bravado rushed out of him to be replaced by grief and shame. The hands that wanted to kill became the resting place for his bowed head.

I then watched my defeated, impulsive brother go to the outer courtyard of Jesus' trial. I ached for him. In a moment, his assurance, his strength, his boldness disappeared. Left behind was a version of my brother I have never seen. Never. In all our years, he has been larger than life. And though I am older, my quieter nature has placed me in his shadow. A place I mostly have not minded. I remember the day I ran to him to tell him I had found Jesus, the promised One. What a moment. So very different from this moment. I am thankful that sleep has found my brother. His grief has been like an ocean wave. Absolutely crushing, all-consuming, unforgiving.

My gaze travels over the rest of my friends. We are only eleven now after losing Judas. The women who have been with us along the way - following the warmth of Jesus, too - have all returned to their homes. Mary Magdalene plans to return to the grave after the Sabbath ends. She and her friends want to properly anoint and wrap the body of Jesus. Things were so rushed after Joseph of Arimathea took his body down from the cross. There was insufficient time to fully honor his body before bringing it to Joseph's burial tomb.

I know Mary followed along. She needed to see where Jesus' body would be placed. She loved him as much as any of us. Jesus literally changed her life. We would never have accepted a woman like her if it had not been for Jesus. His capacity to love obliterated the boundaries we all had in place. The warmth of him invited all to come. Declared all were welcome. And I mean all.

Any person.

Anywhere.

From any walk of life.

With any history.

Of any age.

All welcomed.

All loved.

All valued.

All.

Do you even understand the extravagance of that? Do you even understand? What we have lost is his way of embracing everyone, including everyone, loving everyone. Jesus' way of honoring God and loving others was so fantastically complete and amazingly unrestrained. In his absence, it is no wonder I feel cold.

What will we do now? The sun will rise soon. My friends will wake. I probably will not have slept. It will be a new day, but no one will want to engage it. No one will have the courage to go out. We will continue to sit in our fear, uncertainty, and sorrow. The coldness of this in-between place will paralyze us. What is missing now is Jesus. I long to see him. I need to have him tell us what to do next. I ache to feel his warmth. Because right now, I am not in a good place and there is no one here to tell me everything will be okay.

Suddenly, a strange sense of peace enters the chaos of my thoughts. I marvel at it. Because these emotions should have me in a state of panic. Yet I am calm and thoughtful, and I realize that the peace is telling me something. As I listen, I am embraced by the whisper of something more. Something yet to come. I realize the first hint of morning light is seeping into the room. The new day is approaching and with it comes something more. What it is, I cannot say. But I am sure of its promise. I am feeling warm.

34

TELL THE DISCIPLES

- MARY MAGDALENE -

Mark 16:1-8

I HAVE ONE FINAL gift to give. It cost me dearly. He is worth it.

We started out at sunrise, walking together. Four women on a journey of sadness and dedication. Only on Friday, two days ago, we watched his crucifixion and his life drain from his body. Those were long, unbearable hours. Mine spent bent over on the ground, breathing in dirt as I wept for everything that I was losing: wisdom, freedom, life, hope. When the moment came, his last breaths on earth leaving his ravaged body, darkness closing in though it was only midday, we weren't ready. We simply were not prepared to have him go. We needed him among us. I needed him the most. Yet his life drained away, so excruciatingly final that I needed John's strength to help me stand.

We stayed with him as long as possible; his mother, John, and I. We watched as they took his body down from the cross and a man named Joseph took charge. He and Nicodemus carefully wrapped Jesus' body in spices and linen for burial. Then we followed Joseph and the others to the tomb he had secured for the resting place of the One we thought was the Messiah. At that moment, it did not seem to be the right title for him.

Even so, he meant the world to me and I cried out when they rolled the stone into place, my heart hurting beyond measure. Slowly, everyone left until it was just the three of us. John was holding Mary's arm, supporting her exhausted body. Tears rolled down her face as she asked if I wanted to return with them. I shook my head, didn't speak. I couldn't. But I wanted to stay at the tomb longer, even though it was now guarded by Roman soldiers. Mary and John understood and walked away. I stayed.

It wasn't until several hours later that I found the strength to stand and finally went home. But not before making a promise to Jesus. I told him I would come back after the sabbath. I would return with oils and spices to care for his body and adequately prepare it for its unending rest. It should have been done before the tomb was sealed. It wasn't, and I promised I would return and make it right. and so I have. Accompanied by three other women who lived and walked with Jesus as I did: Mary, Salome, and Joanna. We have not spoken much since greeting each other at dawn. Each of us carries the sacred oils and spices needed for what we will do. I am asking God for strength because I know this will not be easy.

Our footsteps are slow, dragging in the dirt. The heavy relentlessness of grief hangs all around us like a deep fog on a summer morning. I am thinking back on my memories of Jesus. He was an excellent teacher, always using simple illustrations so we could understand the truths that at first seemed complicated, but in the end were not. He would do it with just us, his followers. He would do it with gatherings of all kinds of people. Huge crowds and crowded homes. He would teach the religious leaders, though they didn't want instruction from him and were often offended by what he said. Jesus had such wisdom. Through the years, we learned it sprang from his relationship with God.

I remembered the day I met him. I was an outcast whom no one came near. They were afraid of me. More to the point, they feared what lived inside me. Demons. Seven of them. I could no longer separate myself from them and retreated into a small space inside of myself, protecting what little of me was left. I watched the world through their eyes and saw how evil they were and how much destruction they caused. Then he came. And for once, instead of making others cower in fear, I watched my demons cower. Instinctively, they knew who he was, and he had power over them.

Instead of ignoring me like everyone else, Jesus approached. He saw me, somehow, hiding inside of myself. I am sure of it. He looked so intently at me as my demons screamed at him in fear. Then, with all authority, he told them to leave. And they did. They left. All seven of them. Not one remained to torment me any longer. I was the only one in my body in that beautiful, freeing moment. I marveled at the feeling of it, the freedom. Jesus smiled and invited me to follow him. I did not hesitate.

I am still following him. Though I don't know what that will mean without him. I look into the distance and can see the tomb not so far away. I glance behind me and realize that I have walked far ahead of my companions. Lost in my thoughts, my feet must have taken over, moving at an advanced pace. They have not called me to wait, so I press on. They will catch up. I am grateful for the time alone. As I get closer to the tomb, I can see there are no longer any Roman soldiers standing guard. I panic. Without the soldiers there, how will we move the stone? Where have they gone?

It is mysteriously quiet as I arrive at the tomb. No one is there, but the tomb is open. My heart skips a beat, scared at what this could mean. I look around, desperate for someone to appear and explain what I see. I can make no sense of it and I am trembling. I step closer to look into the tomb and realize a strange light exists. I stop and turn around to look for my friends. They are just coming over the hill and seem surprised to see me standing in front of an open tomb with no one else present. They run the rest of the way. "Mary..." Joanna begins, but has no words to finish.

We are all looking into the tomb with the strange light inside. "Should we go in?" Salome asks.

I am closest to the opening, and at her words, I make my feet move. I duck and step into the tomb, only to be met with the most amazing thing I have ever seen. As one who lived with the darkness of seven demons inside her, the overwhelming goodness of standing in the presence of angels is indescribable. "Don't be alarmed," one of them said to me. "You are looking for Jesus of Nazareth, who was crucified. He isn't here! He is risen from the dead!"

A cry escapes my lips as I try to accept the news he delivers. I can see for myself that Jesus is not in the tomb. I can see it, but my brain cannot comprehend. Seeing my confusion, he continues, "Look, this is where they laid his body." He points to the linen in which his body and head were wrapped. They are stained with his blood, but utterly empty of anybody. I stumble backward from the tomb as I hear the other angel say, "Now go and tell his disciples, including Peter..."

I stare at the astonishment on the faces of my friends. We are slowly beginning to understand what all of this means. No more Roman guards. An open tomb. Angelic messengers. Jesus' body is gone. The words "He is risen" ricochet through my head and travel down to my heart, igniting a new fire where moments before were only the embers of an older, dying fire. "He is risen." The truth of it sits before us and draws out another truth that we had stopped believing. He really was the Messiah. Jesus. The One who saves has been saved, and so are we by association. Saved. All of us. In the startling joy of the moment, I recall the angel's charge as I left the empty tomb, "Go and tell his disciples." I smile. Oh, messenger from heaven, you already have.

35

DOUBT DESTROYED

- THOMAS -

John 20:26-29

I'M NOT A VERY optimistic person. I notice what's bad about a situation, not what's good. I know I'm not the easiest person to be around. Sometimes I think the other guys get a little annoyed with me. I'm always questioning and often irritable.

That's how I feel today. Irritable. More than that, I feel cheated and empty and lost. Everything is in turmoil. When we arrived in Jerusalem, I thought we were heading for victory over Roman oppression. As we walked alongside Jesus, the noise of the crowd was deafening. Everyone was pressing in, wanting to touch him, shouting "Hosanna!" It was the first time that I had felt joy in a long time. That feeling of joy has evaporated. I can't find even one speck of it left in me.

We didn't win. There was no victory, no freedom from Rome. I shouldn't be surprised. It's not like Jesus was trained like a warrior. No, he was trained for a different kind of battle. But we all thought he would win, anyway. When you watch someone walk on water, heal the sick, call demons out of people and raise the dead...even a skeptical person like me believes Jesus can do anything. Instead, he did nothing. He's dead.

Honestly, I don't know why we are sitting in this dark room again...doors locked and windows closed. It's making me edgy. What's the point? He's gone. It's not like he can raise himself from the dead. It's crazy enough to know he could do it for others, but complete insanity to think that he could do what they want me to believe. That Jesus is alive. They say they've seen him. I refuse to believe it.

For me, it's over. We should go home. We should return to doing what we did before he came into our lives. Why did I follow him in the first place? How did I come to believe he was the Messiah? I find I am doubting the past years of ministry and the miracles I shared with him. Perhaps he just fooled us. Am I that gullible?

I look up from my thoughts. Across the room from me, I see Peter, who is a man transformed. A week ago, he wore this constant look of pain. I felt for him. He had the chance to stand up for Jesus, but he denied that he ever knew who Jesus was. But now I see that pain erased, and the light has returned to his eyes.

Next, I see John. Of all of us, John was closest to Jesus. He looks content and thoughtful. He stares off into the distance as if he is looking for something. Maybe he's remembering last week when they say Jesus appeared. I wish I had been with them. But I left because the atmosphere in this room was so oppressive. I needed space to think. When I returned, they told me Jesus had been there. I don't think so. Jesus is not coming back.

My eyes scan across the rest of them. I am struck by the fact that today, a week after they say they saw Jesus, they are happy. I feel something twist inside me. Suddenly, I am a man on the outside, looking in. I find I'd rather not be here with them. Maybe I should leave.

I look down at my feet as I consider a second exit from this gathering, a second exit from this room. I could go and never come back. They can hold on to their conviction that Jesus is alive. I can't. I told them I would only believe if I could see Jesus myself. That's not going to happen.

I've come to a decision. I will stand up, leave this room, and just go my own way. It's easier. I can't stay with them when I don't believe what they say. I'm a simple man. Is it so wrong that I need to see things to believe them? They're all engaged in conversation right now. They probably won't even notice I am leaving.

I wait a few more seconds. Maybe I want to change my mind? I ignore that hope and rise. With my movements, all conversation in the room comes to a stop. I wince. I thought I could leave undetected, but they obviously have seen me. Fine. They can watch me go. I turn toward the door and stop because I'm looking at the impossible. With eyes of compassion, Jesus stands looking at me. Not at everyone else. Just at me. He speaks and his words have immediate effect, "Peace be with you!"

I didn't know how badly I needed to see him, how desperately I needed to hear his voice. He has come for me. "Put your finger here and look at my hands," he says to me as he shows me the nail scars on his hands. "Put your hand into the wound in my side. Don't be faithless any longer. Believe!" My fingers twitch at the invitation, but I don't move. His words to me are enough.

I was ready to walk out on my life as his follower. I was ready to give in to my skepticism and turn my back on it all. I was ready to abandon him because of my lack of faith. I do not lack faith now. I don't even need to touch him. He has healed me in a way that I didn't know I needed healing. I smile at him and say, "My Lord and my God!" With these words, I proclaim who he is. Moments ago, I was ready to leave. He has extended grace. I choose to stay, overwhelmed by the thought that Jesus came back for me.

36

FEEDING FISHERMEN

- PETER -

Luke 5:1-11 | John 21:1-14

IT ALL STARTED WITH that crazy catch of fish years ago. We had been fishing through the night, Andrew, James, John, and I. But after hours and hours of casting our heavy nets into the water, we had nothing to show. So, we gave up and headed to the shore. That was when our lives intersected with a teacher known as Jesus. He was on the beach with a small crowd when our empty boats pulled in. We were weary from the hard work of a long night and barely paid him attention. We focused on tending to our nets and anchoring the boats, then we waded to shore.

The next thing we knew, Jesus was telling us how to fish. Imagine that! A teacher. Telling fishermen how to fish. It seemed absurd. "Now go out whre it is deeper and let down your nets to catch some fish" Who was this guy? What could he possibly know about our trade? Well, absurd or not, it turned out that he was right. We did as he said and immediately had so many fish in our nets that we had trouble hauling them into the boat! Jesus orchestrated a miraculous catch of fish for us that day. It was just the beginning.

We eagerly followed him for three years. I loved him like my brother, and I was sure I would have laid down my life for him. But the truth is, I was not as ready to die as I thought. The chaos on the night soldiers came to arrest him in the garden revealed that I misplaced my bravado. I drew my sword against a perceived enemy out of fear and anger. But it was Jesus who told me to put it away as he healed what I had damaged. I will never forget that moment. How small I felt. How ashamed. How tucked into his shadow I was when I meant to stand tall at his side.

It was brash what I did. It was foolish. And Jesus was neither of those things. I longed to be more like him and was horrified at that moment to find that I still had so far to go. I felt desolate. The worst was yet to come, only we had no idea. Looking back, if we had listened and paid attention, we would have noticed the times he told us his death was at hand. But when you are young and foolish like me, death seems impossible.

Later that night, we regathered in the courtyard outside where Jesus was being held. We were not allowed inside and could only guess what was happening to him. I was in agony, wishing I could think of something to do. How could I possibly help him? I was not ready to give him up! I had so much I wanted to ask him, to learn from him. The raw emotion bottling up inside me made the next moments volatile.

It started with a young servant girl, followed by some random man, and then another. In rapid succession, they all asked about my relationship to Jesus. I panicked. I panicked when Jesus would have been calm and thoughtful, concerned for others. "I don't know him!" I blurted out. I said it not once, not twice, but THREE times. When I could have identified with Jesus, I did not. Instead of standing up for my teacher, mentor, and friend, I did just what Jesus had predicted I would. I denied him three times and then that stupid rooster crowed.

The guilt I carry from that night is heavy. I cannot find peace. Not even here as I sit with friends on the shoreline of a quiet lake, marveling at the truth that he is alive. We saw Jesus die a criminal's death on a cross, but somehow, he has triumphed over death. Since then, we have seen him three times. I find I want to see Jesus now, sitting with us like it used to be. Without warning, I jump up and say to the others as I stride away,

"I'm going out fishing." I hear them scramble behind me and my brother says, "We'll come, too." So, we all climb into our boats and push off from shore: James, John, Philip, Nathanael, Thomas, and my brother Andrew beside me.

We were out for hours. I was completely wrong if I thought this would be a good distraction from my tortured memories. It was miserable. It was hot and there was no wind. We were not catching a thing. Each one of us getting more and more surly with every passing minute. Finally, we gave up and rowed toward shore. I was hungry and angry. Nothing was right. Nothing felt the same without him. We could not even catch fish anymore.

As we got within range of the shore, a person was standing near our campsite. He held up his hand in greeting and yelled, "Fellows, have you caught any fish?" I rolled my eyes and snorted as I heard Andrew's polite answer, "No." The next thing the man said rang strangely in my ears. "Throw out your net on the right-hand side of the boat, and you'll get some!" It transported me to the day I met Jesus. This fishing advice was hauntingly familiar.

As I stood there transfixed by my memory, my friends were quick to do as he said, throwing the nets overboard and immediately feeling the strain from the weight of the fish. I stared at the nets, at the fish, suddenly realizing who was standing on the shore. I heard John say, "It's the Lord!" But I was already out of the boat, in the water, moving as quickly toward shore as I could. I arrived on the beach, wet up to my waist, in awe of the one standing before me. With a gesture toward the fire, he invited us to breakfast.

We ate. Fish and bread, yes. But once again, his presence and words filled our souls more than food could fill our stomachs. Just to be near him, hear his voice, his laughter, was the reassurance we all needed. As I swallowed my last bite, I looked at Jesus to find him thoughtfully considering me. Before I could speak, he said, "Simon son of John, do you love me more than these?" Without hesitation, I boldly answered, "Yes, Lord, you know I love you." What he said next was puzzling to me. "Then feed my lambs."

I sat in the silence, not knowing how to respond. Then he spoke again. "Simon son of John, do you love me?" The same question was asked a second time, as if the first had never been queried. I answered a little more slowly, "Yes, Lord, you know I love you." I was watching his face, trying to discern his thinking. His response, like the first, was curious. "Then take care of my sheep."

Still looking intently at me, he said, "Simon, son of John, do you love me?" A third time? Why ask the same question three times? Did he not believe my answer? Was my answer wrong? What exactly did he want from me? Taking a breath to calm my frustration and hurt, my answer was more measured the third time. "Lord, you know everything. You know that I love you." He smiled then, and said again, "Then feed my sheep."

As the last word left his mouth, I felt strangely lighter. I immediately understood what he was offering. Forgiveness. Three times, he extended forgiveness and called me into service, patiently replacing each time I had denied knowing him. What I could not forgive in myself, he lifted away. The weight of guilt was gone, and I stood before him, made new. Looking past my flaws, he called out my potential as a leader. And he gave me a charge, one that is greater than I could have imagined. That he thinks I am capable is humbling beyond measure. But HE is beyond measure. As I look at the approval on his face, I understand that he thinks the same about me.

37

TAKE ROOT

- MARY MAGDALENE -

I LOVE THE WAY he teaches. His parable about the sower still lingers in my mind. It's as if he crafts his stories just for me, though I know they are truly for everyone. What he has done for me is just as extraordinary as the words he uses to reveal his kingdom. I am growing now, face towards the sun, like the most glorious of sunflower fields. But it wasn't always so.

When he first entered my life, I was rootless, dying. Like the seeds in his parable, I simply had not come to rest in a place where I could grow. Trampled underfoot, withering in the heat of the sun, choked out by weeds and thorns—these fates fit one aspect of my life or another. A woman in a world of men, I was collateral damage, just like the seeds that fell beyond the sanctuary of the soil.

The brokenness and desperation of that time is far behind me, but the memory is fresh, and the pain still stings. My healing began with Jesus and the words he spoke over me. It continued in the way he welcomed me into his ministry and trusted me with some of the most important truths. It solidified every time he called me by name—Mary.

Like a gardener tending to a wilting plant, the time I spent in his discipleship community allowed him to nurture me toward health and I grew. My roots found soil instead of rocks and an unyielding path. I flourished in the shade of those who blocked the harshest heat from the sun until I could bear it on my own. With the help of the others, I learned to protect

147

my heart from the lies of those who sought to choke me. And I grew stronger. Jesus spoke life into me. My thirsty soul received it and slowly believed everything he said.

Today we are gathered for a meal. It has been three weeks since his resurrection and the air is thick with his presence, giving weight to the moment. Through the years, I have learned to pay attention in spaces like this. He speaks of things that seem to be imminent. I have been listening closely and I know his time with us is truly coming to an end. I wonder what it will be like to live life without the nurturing he brings to all of us? But because of the time spent with him and the others, I stand with my face to the Son. I am confident that my roots are deep enough now to withstand anything.

Author's Note

I wrote these stories in a random order over nine years, the first one in 2014 (Redeemed). Some of them, notably the Advent/Christmas and Lent/Easter stories, were requested for worship services at Plymouth Covenant Church in Plymouth, MN and Faith Covenant Church in Burnsville, MN. I served both churches as pastor to kids and families. The rest of the stories were written when I felt inspired to write. This book is the first time I have shared them with others.

I want to include some information on specific stories so you can receive them as I intended them to be received:

A Whisper of More, Lost and Found, and *Take Root*: these stories are pure fiction. They have ties to Scripture, but don't build on actual biblical accounts. We don't know how the disciples spent the day between Jesus' death and resurrection. John 20:19 references that the disciples were "meeting behind locked doors because they were afraid of the Jewish leaders," but this statement occurs after the resurrection. The events of Saturday are up to our imaginations. The servant girl provides perspective on the events of Holy Week from someone who would have been virtually invisible to others. And *Take Root* is simply honoring the journey of Mary Magdalene from complete outcast to devoted follower of Jesus. I expect her story involved emotional and spiritual healing that she received as she traveled with Jesus and the others.

Summoned By Paranoia and *Under the Fig Tree* are stories I did some research to write. In *Summoned*, I wanted to know who the high priest would have been when the wise men came around searching for Jesus. It's tricky, because the year of Jesus' birth is debated, often placed around 6-4 BC. We know Jesus was no longer a baby when the wise men arrived at his home, so I was looking for the high priest around 4-2 BC. That could have been Eleazar ben Boethus (high priest 4-3 BC), whose sister Mariamne was King Herod's fifth wife. I found it an intriguing connection and wrote it into the story.

In *Under the Fig Tree*, I pictured Nathaneal as a scholar. As I was researching him, I came across the possible play on words with "netzer" as a reference both for "branch" and for "Nazareth." As an English major, the wordplay was too tempting to pass up! Into the story it went. There was no exhaustive scholarship on either of these ideas (netzer and Eleazar), so please receive them as interesting but not necessarily definitive.

It is my prayer that these stories have created a longing in you to know more about Jesus. The best place to do that is in the four Gospels: Matthew, Mark, Luke, and John. These men were contemporaries of Jesus, and their eyewitness accounts can be trusted. If you are new to Bible reading, I suggest using a Bible/Bible App in the New Living Translation. It is a solid translation that sounds closest to everyday English. If you're not sure where to start, I recommend John's Gospel. Unless you like the miracle stories—then read Luke. Or, if you have favorite stories from the book, use the Scripture references provided at the beginning of each story to read its complement in the Bible.

About the cover art...

...my daughter, Emma Sosa, painted the oil on canvas painting that became the cover for this book. I was in a difficult season of life that felt like being in a deep, dark valley. I spent considerable time pleading with God for a fast-track way out of the valley, all the while knowing I was meant to walk through it. When Emma sent me a picture of this painting, I knew God was confirming the need to traverse the valley and that he was promising more. The painting is called "sola ossa" which is Latin for "only bones." It reminds me that with God, new life comes, even in a valley. You can read about it in Ezekiel 37.

A word of thanks...

...to my parents for loving me so well; my brothers for being two of my biggest fans; my children Emma and Matteo for helping me see Jesus through their eyes; my writing coach Meg Calvin and her team (Heather Paul and Brent Schebler) for moving this book from my computer into the real world; and to so many of you for your encouragement and support! I am beyond grateful to have so many stellar people in my life!

ABOUT THE AUTHOR

Sara helps people feel more confident in their influence as followers of Jesus. She does this as an author, coach, Family Ministries Pastor, conference-wide Director of Children's Ministries for her denomination, and university professor. She has a Master of Christian Formation from North Park Seminary and a Doctor of Ministry Degree in Church Leadership from Bethel Seminary. When not teaching or writing, you can find her walking her dog, laughing with her two adult children, and dreaming of owning an island off the coast of Scotland. She would love to connect with you at saraheacox.com

www.ingramcontent.com/pod-product-compliance
Lightning Source LLC
Chambersburg PA
CBHW060457300726
48975CB00008B/2547